"Do you think I've been followed?"

Tanner hesitated, then decided he couldn't lie to Sidney. "Yes, I think so."

She shuddered. "I'm surprised Santiago's men didn't take a shot at me when I was standing outside Camella's doorway."

Yeah, that had been troubling him, too. Although it was clear that while Sidney was a target, the goal was to have her influence the outcome of the trial.

Something she couldn't do if she was dead.

Considering the amount of time it would take to bring another judge up to speed, he felt certain Santiago wouldn't want another postponement.

But then why kill Camella? Just to prove to Sidney how vulnerable she was?

The crack of gunfire echoed around them.

"Get down!" he shouted at Sidney, while he frantically searched for where the gunman was shooting from.

"Lilly!" she cried hoarsely.

"I know." Tanner was thankful the SUV hadn't been hit. At least, not yet. He wrenched the steering wheel and went cross-country, rocking and rolling over the rough terrain, toward the small town of Wellington, Colorado.

He was desperate to find a safe place...

Laura Scott has always loved romance and read faith-based books by Grace Livingston Hill in her teenage years. She's thrilled to have been given the opportunity to retire from thirty-eight years of nursing to become a full-time author. Laura has published over thirty books for Love Inspired Suspense. She has two adult children and lives in Milwaukee Wisconsin, with her husband of thirty-five years. Please visit Laura at laurascottbooks.com, as she loves to hear from her readers.

Books by Laura Scott

Love Inspired Suspense

Justice Seekers

Soldier's Christmas Secrets
Guarded by the Soldier
Wyoming Mountain Escape
Hiding His Holiday Witness
Rocky Mountain Standoff

Callahan Confidential

Shielding His Christmas Witness
The Only Witness
Christmas Amnesia
Shattered Lullaby
Primary Suspect
Protecting His Secret Son

Visit the Author Profile page
at LoveInspired.com for more titles.

ROCKY MOUNTAIN STANDOFF

LAURA SCOTT

LOVE INSPIRED SUSPENSE

INSPIRATIONAL ROMANCE

LOVE INSPIRED® SUSPENSE
INSPIRATIONAL ROMANCE

Recycling programs
for this product may
not exist in your area.

ISBN-13: 978-1-335-73597-3

Rocky Mountain Standoff

Copyright © 2021 by Laura Iding

This edition published by arrangement with Harlequin Books S.A.

For questions and comments about the quality of this book, please contact us
at CustomerService@Harlequin.com.

Love Inspired
22 Adelaide St. West, 40th Floor
Toronto, Ontario M5H 4E3, Canada
www.LoveInspired.com

Printed in U.S.A.

My brethren, count it all joy
when ye fall into divers temptations; Knowing this,
that the trying of your faith worketh patience.
—James 1:2–3

This book is dedicated to fellow author Christa Sinclair.
Thanks for being a great friend and champion!

ONE

Cheyenne Federal Criminal Court Judge Sidney Logan shifted Lilly, her soon-to-be adopted six-month-old foster child, up on her hip as she knocked again. Where was Camella? Granted, today Sidney had been running behind, but she abhorred being late, especially for court.

And it wasn't like her nanny not to respond. Shivering in the cold January wind coming off the Rocky Mountains, she rapped again, louder. "Camella? Are you in there?"

Still nothing. A niggle of worry burrowed under her skin. Juggling the diaper bag, her purse and the baby, she managed to find the key to Camella's house. She inserted it, then unlocked the door and pushed it open. "Camella? What's wrong? Are you sick?"

A horrible stench forced Sidney to take a step back. Alarm bells trumpeted in her mind. She wanted to flee, to take Lilly far away, but forced herself to walk inside.

Camella, who'd been like a mother to her, and a grandmother to Lilly, was lying on the kitchen floor, her throat slashed from ear to ear, obviously dead.

Run!

Sidney whirled and ran from the house, clutching Lilly close, while struggling to breathe. She quickly opened her car door, did her best to get Lilly secured in her car seat and tossed in the diaper bag and briefcase. She slid behind the wheel of her Jeep, then roared out of the driveway and drove as fast as she dared on the snow-dusted streets.

The horrible image wouldn't leave her mind. What had happened? Who would murder an innocent woman like Camella? And why?

Even as the question echoed, she knew why. The last threatening letter she'd received, albeit four long weeks ago, flashed in her mind.

Manuel Santiago must be found innocent or those you love will suffer.

Her breath hitched in her throat. With trembling fingers, she dialed 911 and explained about Camella Monte's death. The dispatcher wanted her name and contact information, but Sidney hung up on her. There wasn't time for that. Not now. She needed Lilly to be safe. The very next call she made was to Tanner Wilcox, the US Marshal who was once assigned to protect her. She'd heard he was returning to Cheyenne, but wasn't sure when. The trial wasn't for a few days yet.

"Your Honor, it's always nice to hear from you." His slow Texas drawl grated on her nerves, but she ignored it.

"I just found my nanny brutally murdered," she said bluntly. "The Santiago case is scheduled to start Monday and I desperately need your protection as soon as possible, especially for Lilly."

"Where are you?" All traces of his easygoing attitude immediately evaporated.

"I'm driving through Cheyenne away from Camella's home, but I'm due at the federal courthouse in thirty minutes for a pretrial hearing." Despite the heat blasting through the vents, she shivered.

"Do not go to the federal courthouse or return to your place," Tanner ordered, steel underlying his tone. "I want you to meet me at Holiday Park. I'll be there in five minutes."

"O-okay." Logically she knew he was right about not going to the courthouse or heading home. What if Santiago's men were already following her? She glanced at the rearview mirror, but didn't see anything amiss. Would she? Probably not. Her gaze rested on Lilly babbling happily away in her car seat, completely oblivious to the danger surrounding them.

Surrounding *her*. Sidney felt sick knowing that Camella had died because of her.

Because of the upcoming trial. As the presiding judge, she had control of the proceedings. Yet her history proved her to be fair and impartial, while still being tough on crime.

Sidney hated to admit, even to herself, just how afraid she was of Manuel Santiago. Every time she'd seen the man in her courtroom, his dark eyes had seemed to look right through her.

And that was before she'd found Camella dead.

Murdered.

She swallowed a sob and blinked back her tears. Lilly's safety was all that mattered. She wouldn't let the little girl suffer because of her.

Why had she sent Tanner away?

Granted, the trial had been postponed due to a fight between inmates during which Santiago had been injured. At that point, the threats had stopped, so she'd sent Tanner off to do real work rather than babysitting her. Yet now, she couldn't help thinking that if she'd kept Tanner close, the horror of Camella's death would have been avoided.

Camella hadn't deserved to be killed. She was innocent in all of this. Tears pricked Sidney's eyes, but she swiped them away.

Enough. She couldn't go back and change the past. As she approached Holiday Park, she glanced around nervously. The parking lot was large, but the place wasn't crowded on a Wednesday in January. She drove into the parking lot, and immediately noticed a large black SUV parked near the entrance. Seeing Tanner's chiseled features topped by a brown cowboy hat in the driver's seat made her relax her deathlike grip on the steering wheel.

She pulled up and parked near him. In a flash Tanner was out of the SUV and striding around the vehicle toward her. He was tall, lean and handsome, and five years her junior. He was difficult to ignore on a personal level. Not that she was interested in a relationship. After getting rid of her ex-husband, Gary Wells, two years ago, she'd vowed to stay single.

"Get out, we're taking my car," he said tersely.

She wanted to argue but realized Santiago's men might know what she drove. "Okay."

His gaze landed on Lilly and she thought his expression softened for a moment. "Take your daughter—I'll grab the car seat."

She almost corrected him—Lilly wouldn't officially be her daughter until the adoption was finalized at the end of the month—but she figured that wasn't important. She loved Lilly as if she was her own child, and that's all that mattered.

Although being in danger like this threatened her ability to successfully adopt the little girl. Panic squeezed her heart, but she did her best to set it aside. She couldn't worry about that now. After unbuckling Lilly, who was dressed from head to toe in a tiny pink snowsuit, she reached for the diaper bag and briefcase.

"I'll get those for you," Tanner assured her.

She stepped back, clutching Lilly close while glancing furtively over her shoulder. No one had followed her to Holiday Park from what she could tell, but she felt certain Manuel Santiago's men were out there, somewhere.

Watching and waiting for the opportunity to strike.

Tanner hauled out the car seat, pink diaper bag and leather briefcase out, carrying them to his SUV with ease. He quickly secured the car seat, then stepped back so she could buckle in Lilly.

Tanner stood protectively behind her, his musky scent teasing her senses. She felt safe with him guarding her, and never should have sent him away. It was only a matter of time before he gave her an I-told-you-so.

When she finished with Lilly, she stepped back and closed the door. Tanner placed his hand on the small of her back, urging her toward the passenger side of the front seat.

It wasn't until they were both settled in the SUV, and Tanner was back out on the road, that he said, "Tell me what happened."

"I didn't need to be at court until ten thirty this morning. When I knocked on Camella's door, there was no answer. I thought she might be sick, so I used my key to get inside. Th-that's when I found her. She'd been murdered." She put a hand over her stomach, swallowing a surge of bile.

"I'm sorry to make you relive this," Tanner said in a low voice. "But I need to know what you saw."

"C-Camella lying on the floor in the kitchen, her throat slit. Th-there was a lot of blood." Her voice hitched and fresh tears threatened, but she strove to be calm. "I left as quickly as possible, then called 911 to report her death before I reached out to you."

Tanner's expression turned grim. "The local police will want to talk to you."

"I know." She was well aware of how the justice system worked. "I couldn't stay, Tanner, because of Lilly." She glanced back at the baby. "I needed to make her my priority."

"Understandable," Tanner agreed. "We'll arrange for your statement to be taken. But not until we get you and the baby settled someplace safe."

"I need to let my clerk know to cancel Santiago's pretrial hearing." She fumbled for her phone, but Tanner put a hand on her arm.

"Not now," Tanner said.

"I'm the judge," she said with a frown.

"I can't just not show up for my own hearing." If an attorney had done something like that, she'd find him or her in contempt.

"Fine, make the call, but don't say anything more," he warned. "Your life is on the line, Your Honor, and so is Lilly's. That takes priority over proper court etiquette."

He was right. She knew he was right. But that didn't make her feel any better. "I'll make the call quick, without giving too much away."

Tanner didn't argue as she made the call. Becca sounded distraught at the lack of information, but Sidney cut her off. "I have to go. I'll call you later." She disconnected and sighed. "This is because of the Santiago trial." She glanced at him. "Go ahead and say it."

He looked puzzled. "Say what?"

"You told me the danger was still there, despite the lack of threatening notes." She ran a hand through her dark curly hair. "You were right and I was wrong."

"Your Honor—" Tanner began, but she cut him off with a wave of her hand.

"You may as well call me Sidney. My formal title isn't much better than ma'am." He'd ma'am-ed her to death, which made her feel far older than her thirty-six years.

The corner of his mouth kicked up in a small smile. "Listen, I'm here now. I'll protect you and your daughter."

She turned to look at him. "The trial doesn't start until next week."

"That doesn't matter. You're clearly in danger." He frowned. "I should have come earlier. I wasn't aware of the pre-trial hearing happening today."

"My fault," she whispered, feeling sick all over again. "Camella's death is my fault." She glanced once again at the six-month-old baby she loved more than anything in the world. "If something bad happens to Lilly, I'll never forgive myself."

Never.

*   *   *

Tanner was no stranger to guilt. Hadn't he been plagued by the knowledge that being away from Emily had been the reason she'd died in that terrible car crash? Well, that and the fact she'd been leaving him. Which she wouldn't have done if he didn't travel so much.

"Camella's death isn't your fault," he said firmly. "Santiago's men killed her. Not you."

She pressed her lips together but didn't say anything. He knew she was still blaming herself.

Turning his attention to the highway, he decided to head down toward Fort Collins, Colorado, at least for now. He'd spent some time in Colorado a few weeks ago while helping his buddy US Marshal Slade Brooks on a case. Slade had been watching over a witness who'd been in danger related to her need to testify at trial, which wasn't that different than

Tanner's current case of protecting a federal judge.

Except for the added complication of protecting a baby.

He'd known about Lilly, of course—after all, he'd spent almost two weeks with Judge Logan back in early December. He'd been assigned to protect her, but when the threats had stopped and the trial had been postponed, Sidney had made it clear she didn't want or need him hovering over her.

There was no denying the judge was stubborn. Obviously, having protection was disruptive, but he'd tried to be as understanding and inconspicuous as possible.

When the trial had been rescheduled for two weeks early in January, he'd been ordered to return to Cheyenne to guard Sidney. Unfortunately, he'd arrived a day late. He was always a day late, he thought grimly. Not that he'd anticipated Santiago's men would go after Sidney's nanny.

Yet now that Camella Monte had been murdered, he didn't want Sidney to step foot in a courtroom. Or anywhere that wasn't a well-vetted safe house.

She wouldn't like it, but he needed to figure out a way to convince her.

"Where are we going?" Sidney's melodic voice penetrated his thoughts.

"Fort Collins, Colorado." He mentally braced himself for her response and wasn't disappointed.

"That's too far from Cheyenne. We'll never be able to make the trip back and forth to the federal courthouse from there."

"You're not going to the courthouse," he countered. "Santiago's men will likely come after you or your daughter next."

She sent a heart-wrenching glance at Lilly in the back seat. "I know Lilly needs protection. As do I. But don't you see? If I don't preside over this trial, Santiago will get exactly what he wants."

This was the same argument they'd had

back in December. "You can hand the case off to a different judge."

"It's not as if there's a plethora of federal judges in Wyoming. Besides, Santiago can send killers after that judge's family, too." She lifted a hand. "And don't tell me that having a male judge is better, because I refuse to allow my gender to be viewed as a weakness."

Yep, same old arguments. He strove for patience. "Accepting help is not a sign of weakness, Sidney. And a male judge might be better equipped to handle Santiago."

"Handle him how? By standing up to his threats? That's what I'm doing. Any other judge would be in the same predicament. Besides, I've been involved in all the motions and arguments from both the prosecutor and the defense over the past several months. I'm in the best position to preside over the trial. Any other judge, male or female, would be at a distinct disadvantage."

Tanner tried not to sigh. He wasn't a legal expert, so she could be right about the motions and such. But he couldn't stand the idea of anything happening to her, or to Lilly, because the leader of a drug cartel didn't want to go to prison.

Especially since Wyoming still had the death penalty. And the prosecutor had made it clear he was requesting that level of sentencing for Santiago.

Hence the threats.

Although why Santiago's men weren't going after the prosecutor, rather than the judge, was a mystery to him. Well, privately he figured the reason was that Sidney was a woman, and Santiago probably found her easier to intimidate.

Which only made Sidney dig in her heels and refuse to cower to his threats. Obstinate woman.

"We just crossed the border into Colorado." Sidney sent him a narrow glare. "Turn around and go back to Cheyenne. I can accept staying in a safe house, but I need to be close to the courthouse. It's a good forty-five minutes in winter weather between Fort Collins and Cheyenne. Besides, I'll need a change of clothes. I can't wear this pantsuit for several days in a row."

He'd been glad to see she'd worn boots, rather than the high-heeled pumps she favored. "You've already agreed not to go to court today, right?" It took effort to keep his tone even and calm. "May as well sit back and enjoy the ride."

The stubborn set of her jaw indicated she was far from happy. Sidney sat quietly for a few minutes, as the cold, snow-dusted scenery passed them by.

Finally she said, "I was thinking of asking the social worker assigned to Lilly's case to take her somewhere else for a while. Maybe set her up with a new foster family."

He was surprised by her suggestion. "Do you think another foster family can keep her safe from Santiago's men?"

"I...don't know," she admitted in a low, anguished tone. "What do you think, Tanner? Santiago's men managed to find Camella—do you think they have the ability to track Lilly to a new foster family, too?"

It was a really good question. One he didn't know the answer to. "I'm not sure what to say. Personally, I think Lilly is safer with us, especially right now. But once the trial begins, we may want to consider another alternative."

She bit her lip and glanced away, gazing out the passenger-side window. A sniffling noise made him wince. Crying? Was the judge who'd always held her own, no matter what life threw at her, really crying?

He couldn't stand it.

"Hey. It's going to be okay." He reached out to touch her arm. Her shoulder-length, wavy dark hair tangled with his fingers. "We'll figure something out."

"I know." She swiped at her face, turned

toward him and lifted her chin. There was her stubborn side. He preferred it to her tears. "I wish I'd have listened to you back in December."

He couldn't deny he'd been frustrated with her sending him away. Still, no one could have anticipated something like this. That Santiago would have gone after her nanny. If the threats hadn't have stopped, he wouldn't have left no matter what she'd said.

"We should have had you and Lilly under protection for several weeks before the Santiago trial proceedings started up again," he said curtly. "But harping on everything we should have done differently isn't going to help. As soon as we find a safe place to stay, we'll figure out our next steps."

"Okay." She seemed to relax a bit at that statement.

As much as he didn't want to remind her of the murder, he had questions. "Do you mind if I ask why you were taking

Lilly to Camella's house? Don't most people ask their nannies to come to their home?"

"Camella does come to my house when I have early court days, because it's easier for me," she admitted. "On late mornings, like today, I take Lilly there as a way to provide different surroundings, and Camella's home is closer to the park." Her expression clouded. "Do you think Santiago's men know that much detail about my schedule? Or did they simply go after Camella because she was my nanny and just happened to find her alone?"

"I'm not sure. How much is your schedule publicized?"

"It's not posted anywhere online for people to see, but it's not necessarily a secret," Sidney admitted. "And it's not just my schedule they'd have to know, but my routine. The way I usually take Lilly over to Camella's on late court days." She paled. "Do you think I've been followed?"

Tanner hesitated, then decided he couldn't lie to her. "Yes, I think so."

She shuddered. "I'm surprised Santiago's men didn't take a shot at me when I was standing outside Camella's doorway."

Yeah, that had been troubling him, too. Although it was clear that while Sidney was a target, the goal was to have her influence the outcome of the trial.

Something she couldn't do if she was dead.

Considering the amount of time it would take to bring another judge up to speed, he felt certain Santiago wouldn't want another postponement.

But then why kill Camella? Just to prove to Sidney how vulnerable she was?

Maybe, but in his mind, murdering the nanny didn't make any sense. Not if Santiago's men wanted to sway the outcome of the trial.

He shook his head and told himself that mystery wasn't his to solve. His sole responsibility was to keep Sidney and her daughter, Lilly, safe.

And he wouldn't mind some help. Using the hands-free functionality of his SUV, he called his boss, James Crane.

"Things are heating up in Cheyenne," Tanner informed him. "I could use some help."

"I can send Colt Nelson to assist," Crane offered. "Fill me in on what's going on."

Tanner quickly explained about the murder of Camella Monte and how he currently had Judge Logan and her young daughter with him. "We're heading to Fort Collins. Could you ask Colt to meet me there?"

"Yes…" His boss hesitated. "I can free up Slade, too, if needed. I'm sure he'd want to be there for you."

"That's okay—Colt should be good enough for now." Slade Brooks had recently changed positions so that he didn't have to travel as much. Slade was happily engaged to Robyn Lowry, the witness he'd protected in the week before Christmas, and their wedding was scheduled to take place on Valentine's Day. He and Colt were both standing up for their buddy and Tanner was truly happy for them. "Thanks, boss."

"Keep me updated," Crane warned. The guy was known to be a bit of a micro-manager. Yet he'd come through for them in Slade's case, and Tanner had to admit, he'd worked for worse bosses in the past.

And it was kind of cute watching Crane court Robyn's mother, Lucille.

He disconnected the call when the crack of gunfire echoed around them.

"Get down!" he shouted at Sidney, while he frantically searched for where the gunman was shooting from.

"Lilly!" she cried hoarsely.

"I know." Tanner was thankful the SUV hadn't been hit. At least, not yet. He wrenched the steering wheel and went cross-country, rocking and rolling over the rough terrain, toward the small town of Wellington, Colorado.

He was desperate to find a safe place.

TWO

Someone was shooting at them!

Sidney kept her head down but twisted in her seat so she could keep an eye on Lilly. How had Santiago's men found them? Her mind whirled at the possibility that Camella's murder was only the beginning.

That she and Lilly may never be safe again.

Maybe Tanner was right about handing over the Santiago case to another judge. Although the idea of putting anyone else in danger didn't sit well. There was only one judge, an older guy named Marvin Carmichael, who didn't have family living in the area. But she couldn't just toss the case in his lap—that wasn't how things worked. Cases were assigned through a judge-rotation process.

Besides, Santiago could very well have a way to reach family members across state lines. After all, he'd had men follow her into Colorado.

She blinked away the burn of tears. This wasn't the time to melt down. She needed to stay strong.

For Lilly's sake.

"Sidney? You can sit up now." Tanner's calm voice helped to relax her tense muscles. "I think we lost the shooter."

She gazed at the quaint small town they were in. The street was long and lined with businesses, and had recently been covered by a layer of pure white snow. "Where are we?"

"Wellington, Colorado. We're roughly ten miles from Fort Collins."

The area looked nice and quiet. They passed a small motel. "Are we staying here, then?"

Tanner blew out a breath. "Yeah, for

now. I want a safe place to meet with Colt."

She shivered. "What if the gunman followed us?"

Tanner glanced at her as he pulled into the motel parking lot. "I understand your concern. The best I can figure is that someone was watching through binoculars and saw us get onto the interstate. It's a straight shot down from Cheyenne to Fort Collins. They must have found a place to sit and wait for us to show up."

It made sense in a horrific sort of way. "Shouldn't we keep driving?"

"I'm concerned this vehicle has been compromised," Tanner explained. "If they had a scope on that rifle, they could have recorded our license plate number. Colt will have a different set of wheels and we'll use his car to find a new place to stay." He hesitated, then added, "Trust me on this, okay?"

"Okay." Truthfully, she did trust Tanner. More than she trusted anyone else. "I should call my clerk so she takes similar precautions."

"Your clerk is Becca Rice, if I remember correctly," Tanner said. Maybe he thought keeping her talking would help ease the tension. "She seems like a nice lady."

"Becca was Judge Robert Forrester's clerk, too. Before he retired. I was blessed to have been appointed and confirmed to replace him two years ago." Why she was having this inane conversation with Tanner she had no idea. But his tactic, if that's what it was, worked. She felt calmer and more in control.

The way she normally was.

"Becca knew about your previous threats, right? I'm sure she's being careful," Tanner said, bringing the SUV to a stop. "And I'm sure she'd let us know if anyone threatened her."

Once again, Sidney looked back at Lilly. The baby didn't seem to have noticed the gunfire that had thankfully stopped as quickly as it had started. Lilly reached up, trying to grab at the plastic flowers dangling over her head from the handle of the car seat.

Sidney hadn't been one for praying, especially after her ex-husband's infidelity and lies, but she found herself humbly grateful that Lilly hadn't been harmed.

Tanner threw the gearshift into Park. "I want you to get behind the wheel. I'll secure a room, but if you see anything suspicious or concerning, I want you to drive off as quickly as possible, understand?"

She swallowed hard and nodded. "Got it."

Tanner slid out of his seat. She quickly straddled the center console and dropped behind the wheel. Good thing she'd chosen to wear a navy blue pantsuit, rather than a skirt. Her booted feet didn't reach the pedals, forcing her to shift the seat forward several inches.

Gripping the steering wheel, she cast her gaze around the motel parking lot, looking for what, she wasn't quite sure. Something suspicious? Concerning? She was a judge, not a cop.

It wasn't until Tanner returned that Sidney realized she'd been holding her breath. *Silly,* she silently admonished herself. Unclamping her fingers, she once again climbed over the console to return to the passenger seat.

"We're set," Tanner said, sliding behind the wheel. His knee rapped loudly against the steering column, making her wince.

"Sorry, I forgot to put the seat back."

"It's okay." He slid back the seat, rubbed his knee and then reversed out of the parking spot. "Our room is along the back side of the motel."

She nodded, relaxing a bit more as he drove around and pulled up in front of a door with a number *10* on the front.

"Get Lilly—I'll handle the rest," he said.

As before, she unbuckled her daughter from the car seat and held her in her arms, taking a moment to inhale the sweet scent of baby shampoo. Tucking Lilly close, she waited for Tanner to pull out the car seat, the diaper bag and her briefcase.

He handed her one of the keys. After unlocking the door, she held it open so he could carry everything inside. She followed, glad the place was clean, if a tad worn.

When the door closed behind her, Sidney's shoulders slumped—she finally felt safe.

For now.

"I need to call Colt," Tanner said, setting everything down on one of the beds.

She nodded and set the car seat up on the small table so she could put Lilly there. The baby looked around curiously. "I'll need to give her a bottle and some cereal soon."

"I understand." Tanner used the tip of his index finger to send the red rose above Lilly's head swinging back and forth, which made the baby reach up in an attempt to grab it.

For a single guy, Tanner seemed to have a way with kids. Or maybe he was just used to charming the ladies. She couldn't blame Lilly for being unable to resist Tanner's bright blue eyes, tousled brown hair and wide grin.

She had trouble ignoring his handsome looks, as well.

Stop it, she admonished herself. This was not the time to think about her strange attraction to the US Marshal assigned to protect her. Thanks to Gary, she'd given up on men. Her plan was to raise Lilly all on her own.

Tanner was not only too young for her, but also too charming for his own good.

Just like Gary.

Tanner stepped outside the room to make his call. She rummaged through the diaper bag, finding the can of formula, a bottle and box of rice cereal. Lilly began to fuss, making squeaky noises that were rather cute, until they turned into a full-blown wail. Using tap water from the bathroom sink, she made a bottle, then added some formula into a small plastic bowl to mix in the cereal.

Before feeding her, Sidney changed Lilly's wet diaper and then settled on the bed, propping up against the headboard. She set the car seat next to her, so Lilly could sit up to eat her cereal, as she didn't have access to a high chair.

The baby preferred the bottle but opened her mouth like a fish to take in the cereal. When the cereal was gone, Sidney wiped Lilly's face, took the little girl into her arms and gave her the bottle.

She smiled down at Lilly, loving everything about being a mother. Even the rough nights, especially after Lilly's open-heart surgery, when the baby had woken every few hours to be fed.

Difficult to handle alone, especially when she'd had to return to work after eight weeks for a previous case, but extremely rewarding. Lilly had been passed over by another couple for adoption because of her medical needs. The minute the baby had required open-heart surgery shortly after she was born, the adoption had been put on hold. Sidney had stepped up to foster Lilly, who had recovered nicely and was doing great.

"Their loss is my gain, little one," she whispered, running her fingertip down Lilly's satiny cheek. The idea of the baby being in danger was sobering. What should she do? Call Tabitha, Lilly's social worker? She couldn't help but worry that Santiago's men might find Lilly with another foster family.

The way they'd found Camella.

Sidney momentarily closed her eyes and rested her cheek on Lilly's dark fuzzy hair. She absolutely needed to know the baby was safe.

And for now, staying with her under Tanner's protection was the best way to accomplish that.

"I didn't hear her cry," Tanner said from the doorway.

She glanced up. "No, but she started gnawing on her fist and making noises, which are clues she's hungry."

Tanner's gaze lingered on the baby, then he shifted to look at her. "Colt will be here in ten minutes. We'll make a new game plan then."

"Okay." She tried to smile, but it felt more like a grimace. "I'll need to call Becca again, to let her know what time to reschedule the hearing."

"Soon," Tanner promised. He looked at Lilly again. "We're going to keep you both safe."

"I believe you." Tanner had done a great job so far. She had never met Colt, but certainly having another marshal around for protection couldn't hurt.

She just hoped she was making the right decision to keep Lilly here with her, rather than dropping her off with another foster family. She could almost hear Tabitha scolding her over the choice she'd made.

But Tabitha Walker didn't know about Santiago. About how he'd do anything, kill anyone who got in his way. Including finding Lilly with a new foster family.

Sidney knew putting her life on the line was one thing, but this sweet little girl shouldn't suffer because she was a judge.

Or, more specifically, because her job was to preside over Santiago's trial.

Tanner found it difficult to remember Sidney as the rather obstinate judge he'd protected during court several weeks ago while he watched this beautiful woman feeding her baby. The way Sidney took command in the courtroom was the opposite of seeing her cooing over the infant.

Forcing away his gaze, he glanced at his watch. Colt would be here any minute, and they absolutely needed a plan. He thought again about how Lilly complicated things. Not that he minded protecting a baby, but what would they do with her once Sidney returned to the courtroom?

Because he felt certain that was the judge's plan. Despite how much he didn't like it, he knew there was no way Sidney would allow Manuel Santiago to get away with murder.

And honestly? He couldn't blame her.

If a judge caved to this sort of intimidation, where would it end? Other criminals with deep pockets would enthusiastically follow suit.

No, Manuel Santiago had to be held accountable for his crimes. Not just for moving drugs up from the border through Texas, Arizona, New Mexico, Colorado and Wyoming. And wherever else his mules took them.

But for the multiple counts of murder that had been attributed to him. Three previous murders of cartel members that had been uncovered, and now a fourth non-cartel member.

Camella Monte.

Tanner wondered how Santiago's men had figured out about Lilly and that Sidney had a nanny. Those closest to Sidney obviously knew, like Becca Rice, her clerk, and maybe even some of the other court employees. But Sidney hadn't said much to him back then, preferring to keep her private life quiet.

So how had Santiago found out?

Through his defense lawyer? The moment Tanner had laid eyes on Quincy Andrews, he'd instantly despised the man. He was your typical slick lawyer, protesting the innocence of his client, whom he had to know was guilty, based on the proof Tanner had heard about.

Yet when Sidney—er, Judge Logan—had suggested Quincy Andrews work with the prosecutor, Darnell Chance, on some sort of deal, the sleazy lawyer had point-blank refused, claiming his client wanted his day in court and would be found innocent of these crimes he was accused of committing.

It was the very next day that the first threat against Sidney had been delivered. The threats had been subtle at first, but became increasingly venomous until a jailhouse brawl injuring Santiago had caused the trial to be postponed until January.

Putting an abrupt end to the threats. Until now.

Clearly an intimidation tactic, one that had now progressed to murder.

He saw Colt outside and strode to the door to let him in. "Thanks for coming."

"Not a problem," Colt said. He glanced around the empty motel room. "No food?"

Tanner inwardly sighed. Granted it was lunchtime, but Colt was constantly all about food. "I figured you'd stop and grab something along the way."

Colt rubbed his abdomen. Considering the amount of chow the guy put away, he was surprisingly lean. "I would have, but you said it was urgent."

"Doesn't matter," Tanner said, waving his hand impatiently. "We're not staying here—too close to the location of the shooter. We need another safe house."

Colt stroked his chin thoughtfully. "There's a cabin in Red Feather Lakes we can use. But the road going through the national forest will be dicey in the snow."

He rather liked the idea of a secluded cabin. "I'm sure your SUV has four-wheel drive, just like mine, right?"

"Right. And chains, too." Colt frowned. "Are we trading cars?"

"Yep." Tanner grinned. "At least mine is clean. I'm sure yours is full of fast-food wrappers."

"I thought we were going to find a location closer to Cheyenne?" Sidney asked.

Colt turned to look at her, his eyes widening a bit when he saw the baby. "Hi, uh, Your Honor."

"Call me Sidney." She pinned Tanner

with a narrow glare. "You said we'd stay close to Cheyenne."

"Look, we need at least a few hours to figure out how to keep you and Lilly safe if you're going to return to the courtroom." He tried to keep his tone reasonable, but her stubbornness grated on him. "It's already past eleven o'clock in the morning. We need to hit the road, pick up something to eat and find a safe place for the night. From there we'll figure out how to get you back into the courtroom."

She held his gaze for a long moment. "I'm not exactly dressed for camping in the wilderness."

"I understand, but you are wearing snow boots."

Her eyes narrowed, but then she caved. "Fine, but next time, include me in the decision making."

"Yes, ma'am."

Her green eyes flashed. "I told you not to call me *ma'am*."

Tanner lifted his gaze to the ceiling,

seeking strength. "I'll try to remember, *Sidney*. Now if you're ready, let's hit the road."

Sidney stepped back from the doorway, still holding the baby. He grabbed the infant carrier, the diaper bag and her briefcase. He wondered if she had information about Santiago's upcoming trial in there, then reminded himself it didn't matter.

He wasn't involved in the case.

Back outside, he found Colt pulling empty wrappers from his SUV. Rolling his eyes, Tanner buckled the infant seat in the back.

"I'll need your keys," Colt said. "And once I get a new ride, I'll join you in Red Feathers."

"Sounds good." Tanner dropped the keys into his hand. "Give me the location of the cabin."

Colt pulled out his phone and rattled off the directions. Tanner committed them to memory, then slid behind the wheel.

"I'll catch up with you soon," Colt promised.

"Thanks," Tanner said, glad to have friends and fellow marshals he could count on in a pinch.

From her perch in the passenger seat, Sidney spent a lot of time gazing out the windows. They grabbed fast food on the way, and ate their sandwiches in the car. It didn't take long for them head through the forest. The snow that had fallen overnight was bright and white, covering the tree branches and creating a winter wonderland.

"It's really beautiful here," Sidney murmured. "I haven't spent much time in the mountains over the last year."

He wanted to ask why, but the ringing of his phone caught his attention. Colt's number was on the screen, so he pushed the talk button.

"What's up?"

"Someone took another shot at your vehicle. I'm fine, but the rear window has been shattered." Colt's tone was clipped. "It's going to take me longer than planned to meet up with you."

"Be careful," Tanner warned.

"Will do." Colt clicked off.

A chill snaked down Tanner's spine. If they hadn't switched rides, Lilly might have been injured, by glass or a bullet.

Or worse.

THREE

An overwhelming wave of relief washed over Sidney once Tanner pulled to a stop in front of a rustic cabin in Red Feather Lakes. The place looked charming, yet isolated, but surprisingly, made her feel safe.

At least for now.

Knowing Colt had taken more gunfire was more than a little concerning. She'd thought Tanner might be overreacting by changing vehicles, but apparently not.

Bad enough she and Lilly were in danger, but now both Colt and Tanner were putting their lives on the line, too.

Her chest tightened with fear. The threats and danger would stop once the trial was over.

Wouldn't they?

She slid from the SUV to unbuckle Lilly from the car seat. They had a routine now, and she knew Tanner would insist on carrying everything into the cabin.

The interior was clean, but rather chilly. What she wouldn't have given for a warm sweater and a pair of jeans. She told herself to get over it.

After setting down the car seat, the diaper bag and briefcase, Tanner crossed over to the woodburning stove.

"It'll warm up in here soon," he promised as he made a fire.

"I know." She blew on her fingers and rubbed her hands together. The rustic cabin gave her a strange sense of peace. Glancing at the snow outside, she thought it might be nice to bring Lilly back here, once the trial was over. By then, she'd definitely need a vacation.

True to his word, the interior of the cabin warmed up enough that Sidney could shed her coat, and then she took

Lilly out of her pink snowsuit. The baby waved her arms around enthusiastically, as if enjoying the freedom of not being bundled up.

She set Lilly on a blanket stretched out on the floor and gave her several toys. Because of the surgery, the baby was a little behind in her milestones. She could sit, but hadn't even begun to crawl, and could only roll over one way, not the other. Still, Sidney knew Lilly was doing extremely well considering her early illness.

Tanner checked the interior of the cabin, moving from room to room and making sure the windows were locked and the curtains drawn. "It's snowing," he said, returning to the main living space.

She frowned. "That's going to make getting back to Cheyenne early in the morning difficult. We'll have to leave here extra early."

"I'm well aware of your annoyance of being late," Tanner said dryly. "We'll get there in plenty of time."

"We'd better."

Tanner gave her a mock salute, set his cowboy hat on the closest chair, then dropped down on the floor to begin playing with Lilly. Her irritation faded as she watched with a bemused expression on her face.

"You're awfully good with kids, Tanner."

He glanced up with a chagrined look. "I don't mind kids, and Lilly is very cute. Besides, there isn't much to do until Colt gets here."

"I feel terrible about the window of your SUV being shot." Her brow furrowed. "I owe you a debt of gratitude for insisting we switch vehicles and for bringing us here. It's nice to be safe, even for a short while."

His expression turned somber. "I'm sorry you're going through all this. I know it's been a rough day."

"A rough day" was putting it mildly. Camella's dead body flashed in her mind.

The burger congealed in her stomach. "Yeah, the worst day of my life. Before now, I thought my contentious divorce was bad. Nothing compares to losing Camella."

Tanner eyed her thoughtfully, as Lilly knocked down the stacked of blocks he'd set up for her. With infinite patience he stacked them again. "I remember you mentioning your ex-husband after receiving the first threat. You were convinced he was the one behind it."

She remembered all too well. Gary had not only lied and cheated, but he'd also made their divorce so much more difficult than it needed to be. Which had really irked her since he was the one who'd cheated and had gotten his mistress pregnant. He'd also lied about his job as an EMT—he'd been let go from his position—which is why he'd sued for alimony. As if three years of marriage entitled him to half her paycheck for the next ten years.

In the end, she'd prevailed, but Gary hadn't been at all happy about it. She'd felt certain the threats were his way of getting back at her.

Until the threats began mentioning Santiago himself. And the requirement that he be found not guilty. As if she could change the jury's mind about what they decided.

"Gary is a weasel, but he wouldn't kill anyone. That would take far too much effort." She didn't want to talk about her ex-husband and the poor judgment she'd made in marrying him. "From what I hear, he's still with his new wife and baby, allegedly loving the role of being a stay-at-home father." Gary's new wife was a doctor at the local hospital. Why a smart woman like that had fallen for Gary's charms was a mystery, but then again, hadn't Sidney done the same?

The only difference was that Sidney hadn't dated Gary while he was married to another woman.

Again, not her problem.

Opening the diaper bag, she pulled out cereal and formula. They had a couple of hours until dinner, but she wanted to have everything set up to be prepared.

Since Tanner was still happily playing with Lilly, she pulled her paperwork from her briefcase. She wanted to review the pretrial motions, to keep her mind from reliving the horror of losing Camella.

Her phone rang, and she recognized Becca's number. Relieved to have cell service despite being nestled in the Rocky Mountains, she quickly answered. "Judge Logan."

"Judge, I have the pretrial motions set up for tomorrow morning at nine sharp," Becca said. "Defense counsel made a big deal out of rescheduling, but he eventually agreed since the trial starts on Monday."

"Thanks, Becca." Quincy Andrews tended to make a big deal about everything. Dealing with Santiago's lawyer was exhausting. "I'll be there."

"Okay, let me know if you need anything else," Becca said.

"I will." She disconnected from the line. Feeling Tanner's gaze, she lifted an eyebrow. "We will be at the courtroom tomorrow well before nine, right?" Glancing down at her wrinkled-beyond-recognition navy blue pantsuit, she was glad she always had a change of clothes in her chambers. It was a necessity when having a baby. Lilly had spit up on more than one of her suit jackets.

"Yes, ma— Uh, Sidney." He scooped Lilly into his arms and rose gracefully to his feet. "The little lady needs to be changed."

"Oh, sorry." She jumped to her feet, reaching for the diaper bag, but he waved her off.

"I can do it."

"Are you sure?" Not that she didn't trust him—clearly he was comfortable around kids—but why would any man actually offer to change a dirty diaper?

"Yep. You keep working." He took Lilly over to the sofa, keeping up a steady stream of chatter as he worked.

It was difficult to concentrate on the pretrial motions while Tanner was grinning down at Lilly like a man besotted. His charm was infectious, but she reminded herself she was immune.

Easier said than done.

When he finished, he set the baby back on the floor with her toys, then carried the diaper over to the garbage can. After washing his hands, he turned to her, his blue gaze serious. "I saw the scar on Lilly's chest—what in the world happened to her?"

"Lilly was born with a congenital heart defect, which caused her to need open-heart surgery shortly after her birth." She said the words simply, but at the time it had been a very big deal. She'd just finished her foster training when Tabitha had called with the news of the baby needing placement.

Sidney had jumped at the opportunity, getting to the hospital just before the surgeon had arrived. She'd only had the opportunity to kiss the little girl briefly, before Lilly had been whisked away.

"Wow," Tanner said. "That must have been rough."

She nodded, then shrugged. "Although I wouldn't have Lilly if not for that surgery, since the parents that were going to adopt her backed out because of it."

He scowled. "Who would do something like that?"

She hadn't understood it, either. "Their loss is my gain." Then she sobered. "And now she's in danger because of me."

"Because of Santiago," Tanner corrected firmly. "You have to stop taking this situation solely on your shoulders."

Again, easier said than done. But she didn't argue. Because he was right in that without Santiago, she wouldn't be here with Tanner.

In fact, she wouldn't have met US Marshal Tanner Wilcox at all.

And despite the way she didn't appreciate being attracted to him, she couldn't help but be grateful for this opportunity to know him.

Even for this brief period of time.

Seeing the red scar marring Lilly's soft skin had been a terrible jolt, but now that he knew how Sidney had taken in the little girl despite her illness, his admiration for the judge grew exponentially.

And he already liked her more than he should.

He reminded himself that his job wasn't conducive to relationships, and that he wasn't offering his heart up on a platter again. Emily had smashed it to smithereens, and it had taken him time to piece the vital organ back together again.

The next couple of hours passed slowly.

The snow continued to fall, lightly but with a steadiness that covered the trees, making Red Feather Lakes look like the inside of a snow globe.

Sidney put Lilly in her car seat to feed her, laughing as bits of cereal ended up in Lilly's hair.

His phone rang, and he was glad to see Colt's familiar name on the screen. "Are you okay?"

"Yeah, but I'm glad we switched cars," Colt said dryly. "I wouldn't have wanted Lilly in the back seat when the window shattered."

Tanner wholeheartedly agreed. "How far out are you?"

"Less than thirty minutes. I'm not far, but figured I'd pick up pizza to go. You and Sidney must be hungry, too, right?"

"Sure, I could eat." Tanner smiled wryly. No one went hungry when Colt was involved in a case. He glanced at Sidney. "Anything in particular you don't like on pizza?"

"I like everything except anchovies," she said, wrinkling her nose. "Never understood the allure of putting little fishes on pizza."

"No anchovies," he told Colt. "Otherwise, load it up."

"Will do. Should be there soon. I put the chains on the tires because of the snow."

"Good idea, I'll do the same." He disconnected from the call and stood. "I'll be back in after I put the chains on the tires. I want to be ready just in case."

Sidney nodded, her brow furrowed. "I guess it's good to be prepared in case we have to leave in a hurry."

"Exactly." He drew on his dark coat and settled his cowboy hat on his head. The winter air outside was cold and brisk, but not terribly so.

Putting the chains on the tires didn't take long, since it was something he'd done often enough. Glancing around, he figured he'd wait until Colt arrived to scout out the area.

He wasn't going to leave Sidney and Lilly inside alone for long.

Thankfully Colt arrived within the promised thirty minutes. "We need to eat—the pizza is already getting cold," he announced.

Tanner nodded. Sidney pulled three plates out of the cupboard and set them on the table. Lilly was still on the floor batting at her toys, making Tanner smile.

As they sat to eat, Tanner briefly bowed his head and closed his eyes, silently thanking God for their food and for keeping them safe.

He normally didn't pray out loud, but when he opened his eyes and lifted his head, he caught Sidney's soft gaze on him. The curiosity and hint of admiration in her gaze made his cheeks redden.

Colt had waited patiently for him to finish, which was saying a lot since Colt lived to eat.

"It's still warm," Tanner said, breaking the rather awkward silence as he helped himself to a slice. "Not hot, but warm."

"Cold pizza isn't bad," Colt protested.

"You'll eat anything at any temperature," Tanner replied, feeling compelled to point that out.

"True," Colt agreed.

"Thanks for bringing dinner," Sidney said as she used a fork to eat her pizza while he and Colt simply picked it up with their hands. "It's great."

"No one starves around Colt," Tanner muttered. "Especially not Colt."

Sidney laughed. Tanner realized it was the first time he'd heard her laugh, and silently vowed to get her through this, so she had more opportunities to laugh.

The way she should.

"What's the game plan?" Colt asked between bites.

Tanner glanced at Sidney. She met his gaze head-on.

"I need to be in the Cheyenne federal courthouse by eight thirty tomorrow morning," she said in her authoritarian judge-like voice. "I'd like to leave here by seven if possible."

"Seven?" Colt frowned. "It's still dark then."

Sidney sent a pointed look in Tanner's direction. "I can't be late for my own hearing."

"We can leave by seven," Tanner said evenly. "That's not a problem."

Colt sighed. "Sure. Although I thought the goal was to keep the judge out of the courtroom."

"I have to move forward with this trial," Sidney said firmly. "I refuse to let Santiago get his way by using threats and intimidation."

And murder, Tanner thought.

"Okay, okay." Colt nodded, his gaze resigned. "I get it."

"At least the courthouse has armed deputies and metal detectors," Tanner said. "That should make an attempt against Sidney less likely."

"Should, but remember what happened

in Denver?" Colt took another bite of his pizza. "A man was killed right in front of everyone."

"Wait, are you talking about the Elan Gifford case?" Sidney asked. She stood and took her plate to the sink, glancing back at him with a troubled gaze. "I heard about that. Something about a knife being hidden in a metal knee brace."

"Yes, but we'll make sure the same thing doesn't happen again," Tanner assured her. He finished his pizza and stood. "Do you need any help? I'd like to go out and scout the perimeter of the cabin."

"You want me to tag along?" Colt asked, taking the last slice of pizza as if it might be the final bit of nourishment in his future.

"I want you to stay here and watch over Sidney and the baby," he said. "Keep your phone handy, just in case."

"I can do that." Colt wolfed down the final slice of pizza. "And we'll take turns keeping watch over night, too."

"Thanks." Colt might be a food monger, but he was a great partner, especially in a crisis. Tanner bent down to stack the blocks for Lilly again, then donned his winter gear and cowboy hat. "Be back soon."

"Be careful," Sidney said in a low tone.

Her concern warmed his heart, although logically he knew that her main concern was for him to protect her and Lilly.

Still, he held the compassion in her green eyes close as he went out into the dark night. The clouds overhead didn't allow for any moonlight, but the snow was bright enough to illuminate the area, anyway.

Stepping carefully in his thick hiking boots, he began a wide sweep around the cabin. When he came across a set of footprints in the snow, he froze.

Someone had been there. Recently.

The tiny hairs on the back of his neck rose in alarm when he saw that the footprints led in a circle around the cabin. The same path he was about to make, only these prints had originated from the woods, rather than near the cabin's front door.

Not good.

He pulled out his phone and called Colt. "Get Sidney and Lilly out of there. I found footprints in the snow. Someone's out here."

"Got it," Colt responded tersely.

Tanner retraced his steps back to the cabin, then brushed snow off the SUVs. Thank goodness he'd put the chains on earlier. And Colt's vehicle still had his chains on, too.

There were no footprints here along the front of the cabin, which only made him think the man who'd scoped out the place hadn't wanted to get too close.

The cabin door opened. Tanner rushed forward and took the car seat from Colt's hands, then quickly put it inside the car.

Sidney followed and huddled close.

The minute he had the car seat secure, he stepped back so she could get Lilly buckled in.

That's when he saw the man with a gun.

"Shooter!" he shouted, pulling his weapon and placing himself directly in front of Sidney.

Colt was a step ahead of him, though, and fired his weapon mere seconds before the guy took his shot. The gunfire echoed loudly, but didn't hit its mark.

"Get inside!" Tanner practically picked up Sidney and hauled her around to the other side of the vehicle.

For once she didn't argue, sliding quickly into the passenger seat. Tanner ran around to the driver's side. "Colt, follow us!"

Colt shot again toward the guy, who'd dropped to his haunches in the snow. For a moment Tanner got a clear look at the man's face before the guy turned and took off running.

"Hurry," Tanner urged. No matter how much he wanted to take off after the guy, he couldn't leave Sidney and Lilly alone. And the guy who'd shown himself might not be alone.

He started the engine and headed away from the cabin, just in time to see another man step out from behind a tree. "Get down," he shouted, hitting the gas. He prayed the chains would give them the traction they needed to escape the gunmen.

If not, they'd be sitting ducks, ripe for the picking.

FOUR

Sidney hugged her knees, bracing herself for the worst as gunfire echoed around them. Knowing Lilly was in the back seat made her feel sick to her stomach.

"Are we hit?" Her voice was muffled—she didn't dare lift her head. "Is Lilly okay?"

"She's fine. We're not hit, but you need to stay down." Tanner's voice was tense, and she felt the SUV chugging faithfully through the snow. Remembering how Tanner had prayed before dinner made her hope he was praying again now.

"Colt?" She listened as Tanner called his fellow marshal using the hands free function of the SUV. "You okay?"

"Yeah, right behind you."

She let out a pent-up breath, grateful that Colt was okay. Had Santiago sent those men to scare her? If so, his ploy was working.

She'd never been so afraid. Except when she'd found Camella dead.

Closing her mind against the image, she concentrated on taking slow deep breaths. More than anything, she wanted to turn around and check on Lilly.

As if he'd read the direction of her thoughts, Tanner said, "You can sit up. We should be safe, now."

"Tanner, let me know if you need anything, okay?"

"Got it." He disconnected from the call.

She sat up and spun to check on Lilly so fast, she felt a bit dizzy. Then she nearly wept in relief when she saw Lilly had fallen asleep.

"Thank you, Tanner." Her voice came out as a hoarse croak. "I know we wouldn't be safe if not for you." Then she quickly added, "And Colt."

"That was a close call." Tanner's expression was grim. "If I hadn't gone out when I did..."

She swallowed hard. "I know."

"But you're still going to the courthouse in the morning." It was a statement, not a question.

"I have to." She wouldn't—couldn't—let Santiago get away with this.

Tanner nodded. "I was thinking Laramie is a good place to spend the night."

Laramie was closer to Cheyenne than Red Feathers, although not by a lot. She nodded. "That sounds good."

He called Colt back. "We're going to Laramie. Maybe touch base with Crane, see if he can find a safe place for us to stay."

"Sure thing," Colt readily agreed. "I'll be in touch."

She tensed. "Do you think it's wise to call your boss?"

He glanced at her. "We need back up from the US Marshals Service, Sidney. I can't risk another snafu like we just experienced in Red Feathers."

"Okay." She couldn't find fault with his logic. Seeing the man with a gun emerging from the bushes had nearly stopped her heart. She still wasn't sure how Tanner had managed to evade him.

They drove in silence for several long minutes. Then Colt called back. "We have adjoining rooms in a motel near a restaurant."

"I hope you didn't pick that one because of your desire to eat," Tanner drawled.

"I didn't pick the place, Crane did," Colt protested.

"Yeah, sure." Tanner didn't sound convinced. "Okay, keep covering my tail until we hit the city limits. Then we'll split up, so you can secure the rooms for us."

"Not a problem." Colt disconnected from the call.

"The prison is located in Laramie." The thought hit her out of nowhere.

Tanner glanced at her. "But Santiago is being held in the Cheyenne county jail, throughout the duration of the trial, right?"

She slowly nodded. "Yes. It's just, I don't know, rather creepy to be in the same city where Santiago has been held for the past few months."

Tanner reached out and gently squeezed her hand. "I'll keep you and Lilly safe."

She clung to his hand like a lifeline, soaking up his warmth. "I know. I'm not sure what's wrong with me. I'm not usually this emotional."

He tightened his grip on her fingers. "Give yourself a break, Sidney. You've been through a lot. These past few hours would put anyone on edge."

Tanner was right. Still, she prided herself on being cool, calm and collected. Hadn't Gary accused her of being unemotional? As she glanced back over her shoulder to check on her sleeping baby, she realized she had been a bit distant from Gary.

It wasn't until she'd held Lilly in her arms and had seen that the tiny girl was totally dependent on Sidney for her very survival that she'd been overwhelmed with emotion.

Love, compassion, caring, fear, worry and joy. Oh, so much joy.

For the first time, she was forced to admit that maybe she hadn't loved Gary the way she should have. With her entire heart.

Then again, she didn't think it was an excuse for him to lie and cheat, either.

Tanner held her hand until they reached the Laramie city limits. Then he released her to call Colt. "Okay, buddy. You're up."

"Got your back," Colt responded. "Stay tuned." He disconnected from the call.

"You two get along really well."

Tanner grinned. "Yeah, we've helped each other out of a few tight spots. Along with another friend of ours, Slade Brooks."

Sidney thought it would be nice to have close friends like that. Oh, she had a few, but being a judge seemed to intimidate some people. And after her divorce, she'd found it difficult to continue her friendships with other couples. She was always the odd person out, and it was easier to stay home than to field questions about who she was seeing—no one—or what Gary was up to... The answer to that was that she couldn't care less.

Focusing on the road, she noted Tanner was driving past the prison. She eyed the high barbed-wire walls and guard tower. Seeing the desolate place made it easy to understand why Santiago was so desperate to get out.

Then again, he'd made the decision to lead a life of crime.

No, she refused to feel sorry for the man who'd likely arranged Camella's murder. Her job was to adjudicate a fair and impartial trial based on law.

Nothing more.

She startled when Tanner's phone rang. He hit the speaker button. "Hey, Colt."

"I have the rooms and keys, no need to stop in at the lobby. It's nothing fancy," Colt warned as he gave them the name and the address. "We're in rooms fifteen and sixteen, which are around back."

"Perfect, thanks." Tanner disconnected from the call and turned around to head back the way they'd come.

Sidney was relieved when Tanner pulled up next to Colt's SUV. The hour was close to midnight, and she really needed to get some sleep.

The only good thing about being in Laramie was that it was a little closer to Cheyenne, only fifty miles via the interstate.

Sidney gathered Lilly from her car seat, the little girl crying out in protest. "Shh," she whispered. "It's okay."

Colt opened the door, apparently hearing Lilly. "Come in, we have connecting rooms."

"Thanks." She ducked inside the room, grateful to be out of the cold.

Tanner grabbed their things, including the car seat, and hauled everything inside. Colt had opened the connecting doors between the rooms. Tanner stepped through the doorway and set the car seat on the small table.

"Thanks." Sidney shrugged out of her coat and tried to soothe the baby, who was not happy at being woken up.

"You need a bottle?" Tanner asked, peering into the diaper bag. "I can make one for you."

"That would be great." She appreciated his willingness to help as she did her best to rock Lilly back to sleep. She could just imagine the complaints of a crying baby going to the motel manager.

The bottle worked, and she gratefully sank onto the bed. When Lilly fell asleep, she carefully tucked the baby into the infant seat.

"Everything okay?" Tanner whispered from the doorway.

She nodded. "Yes, thanks. Don't forget, I want to leave by seven. Court starts at nine and I want to be there early."

"I remember." Tanner hesitated, then added, "Good night."

"Good night." He closed his side of the connecting door, not all the way, but enough to give her some privacy. She washed up in the bathroom, took off her suit jacket, keeping on the blouse, then crawled into bed.

For the first time in her entire career, as a prosecutor and now a judge, Sidney wasn't looking forward to going to court.

Knowing Tanner and Colt would be with her the entire time, was the only way she could relax enough to fall asleep.

"You want to take the first watch? Or the second?" Colt looked at him expectantly.

"The first." He was too wired from the

near miss at Red Feathers to sleep. "If that's okay."

"Fine with me. I can always sleep." Colt stretched out on the bed, covering his face with his cowboy hat.

Tanner sat in the darkness, listening to the muffled sounds outside the motel. The face of the man crouching near the trees, before he'd run off, was etched in his mind. Too bad he couldn't sketch, or he'd try to capture his image on paper.

What he needed to do was to look through mug shots of any known associates to Manuel Santiago to see if he could ID the man. If they could prove Santiago had sent thugs after the judge, the district attorney would file additional charges.

And put Santiago away for a very long time.

But proof wasn't easy to obtain. Sure, he knew very well that Camella had been murdered by Santiago's men, but without proof, she was just another victim of a home invasion.

The biggest question of all was how on earth Santiago was feeding information to his men? The guy was being held in jail, as a previous judge, not Sidney, had refused to grant him parole.

The lawyer? As much as Tanner didn't like the guy, he couldn't imagine a lawyer would stoop so low as to help arrange hits and carry out threats against innocent people.

Especially against a judge.

All phone calls from prisoners were monitored, so he knew that wasn't the source. Maybe the lawyer provided notes to go back and forth? That was also against the rules, but Tanner knew anything was possible.

He made a mental note to ask Crane to dig into the background of Quincy Andrews, Santiago's lawyer. From what Tanner knew, the guy was the most likely source of information leaking from Santiago's jail cell.

It was a leak that needed to be plugged

and quickly. Before anything else could happen.

When three hours had passed, he woke Colt and took his turn to sleep. Normally, he didn't have trouble sleeping, but being responsible for a beautiful judge and an innocent baby weighed heavily on his shoulders.

There had already been way too many near misses for his piece of mind.

Finally, Tanner put his worries into God's hands, and quieted his mind by reciting prayers. He must have fallen asleep because Colt's hand on his arm brought him upright.

"What's wrong?" he croaked.

"Nothing." Colt eyed him warily. "A little on edge, aren't you? It's six thirty. Bathroom's all yours."

"Thanks. Is Sidney awake?" He yawned, the measly three hours of sleep not nearly enough to refresh him.

"Yeah, just heard the baby crying." Colt hesitated, then added, "I ordered breakfast from the restaurant across the street. Should be here any minute."

"Of course you did," Tanner muttered as he staggered to the shower. Food was fine, but he'd need an entire gallon of coffee to keep himself awake throughout the day.

One thing about guarding a judge was that listening to legal discussions all day could be incredibly boring.

Not that he planned on voicing his opinion to Sidney. Watching her at the bench, he saw that she clearly took her role very seriously and seemed to have an in-depth knowledge of the law.

Who else used the word *plethora*?

Hearing her say it had made him want to smile.

When he emerged from the bathroom, he was grateful to see Colt had left him a cup of coffee. He practically inhaled the brew, then followed his nose through the connecting door, appreciating the enticing scent of bacon and eggs. And coffee.

A shaft of jealousy hit hard when he saw Colt and Sidney sitting together at the small table sharing breakfast. Annoyed with himself for the juvenile response, he forced a smile. "Save any for me?" He kept his tone light and teasing.

Colt nodded and swallowed a mouthful of food. "I left you coffee, didn't I?"

"You did, thanks." He glanced down to where Lilly was sitting and playing on the floor. "I must have slept more soundly than I thought. I never heard her cry."

"I didn't let her cry for long," Sidney said with a smile. "She was pretty good, all things considered."

"Here, Tanner, take my seat." Colt grabbed a strip of bacon, then stood. "I'm finished."

Tanner nodded and moved over to sit near Sidney, their knees gently bumping in the process. "Sorry."

Sidney waved her hand. "No need to apologize. But as soon as you're finished eating, we really need to leave. I need time to change my clothes when we get there."

He inwardly sighed. Just because he sometimes ran late, didn't mean she needed to remind him every single time. "I know how you feel about being to court on time, Sidney. It won't take me long to eat." He forked in eggs and ate some bacon. A quick glance around her room confirmed that she was already packed and ready to go.

"I know. And it shouldn't take more than an hour to get to Cheyenne. I mean, the plows would have cleared the inter-state, right?" Her smile was lopsided. "I guess I'm a bit nervous."

"No reason to be worried about your safety." He knew she was thinking about the gunfire they'd narrowly escaped yes-terday. "We weren't followed to Laramie, and I'm sure we'll get to Cheyenne with-out a problem."

"Thanks, Tanner."

"You're welcome." He belatedly realized he'd forgotten to pray before eating. He sent up a silent apology and a quick thanks for the food. Tanner had noticed Sidney hadn't mentioned anything about her faith, and made a mental note to bring it up at some point.

For Lilly's sake, as well as Sidney's.

As soon as Tanner finished eating, he quickly hauled her things out to the SUV. Despite Sidney's fears to the contrary, he had them on the road by seven o'clock.

Colt drove behind him, covering their tail. Lilly babbled as the SUV ate up the miles. The roads were clear, although there were a few areas of drifting from the cold Wyoming wind.

When he pulled into the parking lot of the federal courthouse in Cheyenne, he glanced at her. "We're taking Lilly inside?"

"Yes." Sidney flushed. "I know it's unusual, but keeping her in my chambers is the only way I know she'll be safe."

Tanner hesitated. "Sidney, normally I'd

be happy to watch her while you're behind the bench, but my job is to keep you safe."

"I know. That's why I asked Colt to come into the courtroom with me instead." She shot him a quick anxious glance. "Please don't argue with me, Tanner. For one thing, you're great with kids. And for another, well, I feel much better knowing you're watching over my daughter."

He was touched by her faith in his abilities. Although there was a part of him that didn't want Colt to be the one watching over Sidney. It was a ridiculous reaction, as Colt was a great marshal. "Okay, that's fine. With all the security at the courthouse, you should be safe enough."

She nodded without saying anything more.

Getting them all through the metal detectors and security took longer than he could have imagined with a baby, car seat, diaper bag, not to mention Sidney's briefcase. And his and Colt's weapons. But soon they were in the elevator riding up to the third floor.

Tanner carried Lilly in her car seat as Sidney led the way to her chambers. Colt spoke in a low tone. "You okay with the plan?"

"Yeah." He glanced at his buddy. "I trust you to keep her safe."

"With my life," Colt promised. They weren't just words—Tanner knew full well his buddy meant them with every fiber of his being.

The same way Tanner would protect Lilly, Sidney or anyone else assigned to his detail, with his life, too. It was the oath they took when they donned the badge.

"I think maybe I should live in my chambers for the duration of the trial," Sidney said after returning from the bathroom, where she'd changed into a new pantsuit. And she'd replaced the snow boots with low heels. She drew her robe over her clothes, which made him wonder why she bothered to wear business attire. "Easier than getting through security twice a day."

It wasn't a half-bad idea. He'd roughed it in worse places. The suite had a private bathroom and a small coffeepot. He gestured to it. "Mind if I make some?"

"Help yourself." Sidney was in full judge mode now, taking papers out of her briefcase and scanning them. When there was a brief knock at her door, she straightened and called, "Come in."

"Judge Logan?" Becca Rice poked her head in. "The attorneys are present."

"I'll be right there." Sidney waited until Becca retreated, then turned to pick up Lilly. She gave the infant a hug and a kiss before meeting Tanner's gaze. "Thanks for keeping my baby safe, Tanner."

"Always." He reached over and gently took the infant from her arms. Sidney ran a hand down the front of her robe, then walked through the door, with Colt on her heels.

Tanner watched them leave, knowing all he could do was to protect Lilly while praying God would keep them all safe.

FIVE

Sidney kept her head held high, a serious and hopefully judge-like expression on her face as she took her seat behind the bench. Once she was seated, everyone else sat, as well. When she'd first become a judge, the protocol of standing for her had made her feel silly and more important than she actually was. But now, two years into her position, she'd grown accustomed to the formality.

She focused on the two attorneys, defense counsel Quincy Andrews and federal prosecutor Darnell Chance. Both men were dressed in suits and ties, although Quincy's suit looked as if it cost ten times what she imagined Darnell had paid.

The well-paid life of a criminal defense lawyer.

"I understand you both have motions to bring before the court?"

"Yes, Your Honor," both men replied.

"Okay, then I will hear the defense motions first." She glanced at Quincy Andrews. The lawyer bent over to stay something to his client, then rose to his feet to address the court.

Normally she didn't hear motions with the defendant present in the courtroom, but after Santiago had been injured in jail, his lawyer had pleaded his case, expressing his client's desire to understand all aspects of his trial.

It was highly irregular, however she wanted to be fair and impartial in her rulings, so she'd allowed the defendant to be present at the defense table, as long as he didn't speak or interfere with the hearing.

It was a decision she now regretted. Although she avoided looking directly at Santiago, she could feel his dark gaze on her as they went through the motions one by one.

It was hard to imagine Santiago needed to hear all this, yet she wasn't about to underestimate the man, either. Just because he was accused of murder and drug trafficking across state lines didn't mean he wasn't intelligent enough to understand the proceedings. She glanced briefly over at Colt standing off to her right side, his expression neutral as he scanned the room. A sheriff's deputy by the name of Paul Kramer stood to her left, doing the exact same thing.

She was safe here. There was no way Santiago could get to her. So why did she feel so unsettled?

Santiago wanted to intimidate her, no question about it. He was likely staring at her and wondering how she'd reacted to finding Carmella's body.

She suppressed a shiver, refusing to let Santiago think he was accomplishing his mission.

She would preside over his trial, in a fair and impartial manner. No matter what.

Andrews presented his motions first, then she heard the prosecutor's concerns. This involved a lot of back and forth arguing between them. Reviewing them carefully, she then issued her decisions. In the end, she'd found in favor of one motion for each side, denying the other two. It hadn't been her intent to split them down the middle on purpose, but in using previous case law in her decision making, that's how things had shaken out.

She could tell the men weren't happy, but that wasn't her problem, either. They knew the law as well as she did, and often their motions were an attempt to circumvent case law that didn't go in their favor.

"Anything else?" She glanced between the two lawyers. "I assume you're both ready for the trial to begin on Monday?"

"Yes, Your Honor," The prosecutor, Chance said.

"Yes, Your Honor," Quincy Andrews echoed.

"Good. If that's all, gentlemen? Court is adjourned." Sidney pounded her gavel. Everyone in the courtroom stood, and she rose to leave.

Despite her intention to avoid looking at Santiago, her eyes momentarily locked with his. With an effort, she kept her expression neutral, refusing to acknowledge she'd felt his stare like a punch to the gut. Even worse, she continued to feel Santiago's dark gaze boring into her back as she went through the doorway leading directly into her chambers.

Deep down, she knew Santiago was evil, but she didn't dare voice her opinion out loud. Her role was to remain impartial and hold all proceedings to the letter of the law. It wasn't up to her to decide who was innocent or guilty—that was the responsibility of the jury. At least in this case. There were occasions when defense lawyers asked for a judge ruling, rather than a trial, but those instances didn't happen as often.

Thankfully, Quincy Andrews hadn't made such a request. Honestly, Sidney was relieved the responsibility of finding Santiago guilty wouldn't be her decision, but that of the jury.

Entering her chambers, she couldn't help but smile when she saw Tanner and Lilly sitting on the floor playing together. In a heartbeat, the stress of the morning rolled off her shoulders, replaced by a sense of peace.

"Thanks, Tanner, you're so good with her." She shrugged out of her robe and hung it up on the hanger in the small closet. Then she kicked off her heels and slipped on a pair of flats she kept beneath her desk. Looking like a judge was not at all comfortable, even in Wyoming. Glancing at her watch, she was surprised to see it was close to noon. "She'll be looking for a bottle soon."

"Hey, if she gets lunch, we should eat, too," Colt protested.

Tanner ruefully shook his head. "Stop acting like you're starving to death. Before we worry about lunch, what's on your schedule for the rest of the day, Sidney? How late will you need to stay?"

She looked thoughtful. "I have some paperwork I would normally do here, but honestly can probably review from anywhere as long as I have internet access." There were some legal case studies she wanted to review before Monday, especially those related to arguments pertinent to Santiago's case. "I have a couple of minor hearings tomorrow. Give me a few minutes to look over them. It's possible they can be rescheduled until after the trial." The only downside to that plan was the Santiago trial was scheduled to last for two weeks, based on the number of witnesses both sides were presenting.

Two weeks of seeing Santiago's face

in the courtroom. Not something she was looking forward to, yet she felt even worse for the jury. Then again, she fully believed that every single person was entitled to a fair trial.

It was an oath she'd sworn to protect.

Tanner rose from the floor, then picked up Lilly and held her against his chest. The little girl patted his cheeks and babbled something incomprehensible, but the tender smile on Tanner's face melted her heart.

"I'm thinking we should consider finding another safe house," Colt said, interrupting her thoughts. "But we need something for several days, right? Today is Thursday. If there's a way for the judge to avoid being in court tomorrow, we would need to find someplace to stay for the next four nights until the trial starts."

"I was thinking the same thing," Tanner agreed.

"I thought we'd just camp out here," Sidney protested.

"That would maybe work for a day or two, but not four days, and especially not over a weekend. And trust me, sleeping on the hard floor wouldn't be easy," Tanner countered. He eyed Colt. "Would you arrange something for us? I'm sure Crane has resources available throughout the state."

"I could do that," Colt agreed. "But what about lunch?"

"Why don't you bring something here? Sidney will likely need some time to free up her schedule. And we can feed Lilly while we're waiting, too."

"Okay." Colt looked happy to be in charge of the food. "Is Chinese takeout okay for lunch?"

Sidney smiled. "Fine with me."

"Ditto," Tanner agreed.

"Great. I'll be back as soon as I arrange for a place for us to hide out and pick up our food."

"I know you won't forget the food," Tanner said dryly. "But make sure you find a place off-grid. And don't tell me or anyone else where we're going, just create a plan for us to get there." All hint of humor faded from Tanner's gaze. "I don't want any more surprises."

"Me, either." Colt offered a mock salute, then left the room.

Lilly began to fuss. Sidney went over to the diaper bag and pulled out the formula, a bottle and the box of rice cereal. "Can you hold her a minute while I get this ready?"

"Already am." Tanner jostled Lilly in his arms. "Hey, Lilly, do you know the wheels-on-the-bus song?"

Listening to him sing to Lilly while bouncing her around made her want to cry. Ridiculous reaction. She was a federal judge, the youngest ever to take the bench. She couldn't even blame postpartum hormones for the emotional roller coaster she found herself on.

Tanner being handsome, muscular and caring were no reasons to think of him as anything but the US Marshal assigned to her protection detail.

Yet she couldn't deny that watching him with the little girl she hoped would soon be hers, forever, made her dream of a future that was far out of her reach.

Tanner was too young for her and, based on his interactions with Lilly, would obviously want children of his own. Something she couldn't provide. If she was willing to risk her heart again, which she wasn't.

She shook Lilly's bottle with vigor, shrugging off the absurd idea. As soon as Santiago's trial was over, Tanner would move on to his next assignment. She knew full well that US Marshals covered wide territories. Hadn't Tanner gone to Colorado to assist his friend Slade?

Who knew where his next assignment would take him? Could be anywhere.

While she remained in Cheyenne to preside over her next trial.

"Here, I'll give her the bottle. Why don't you make the cereal?" Tanner took the bottle from her fingers and popped it into Lilly's eager mouth. The little girl calmed in his arms, staring raptly up at him.

Sidney could relate. She wouldn't mind gazing at Tanner's handsome features, or staring into his intense crystal-blue eyes, either.

Enough. She made more formula and added it to a small bowl of cereal. Then she dug through the diaper bag to find a jar of vegetables. Lilly seemed to enjoy peas, liking them better than green beans, and Sidney was determined to provide the little girl with a healthy diet, so her heart would continue to grow strong.

While Tanner fed the baby, she quickly straightened her desk. She slid more paperwork into her briefcase and tucked her laptop computer in, as well.

Then she studied her calendar. Satisfied her hearings could be rescheduled without causing an undue delay in justice, she called Becca.

"Yes, Your Honor?" Becca answered.

"Please reschedule everything on my calendar tomorrow for after the Santiago trial," she directed.

There was a brief moment of silence. "Everything?" Becca asked. "Are you taking the day off?"

The question irked her, but Sidney belatedly realized that her being off meant Becca wouldn't have much to do, either. The clerk had a right to know her own schedule. "I'll be preparing for the trial from home, so I won't be in tomorrow."

"Okay, I'll get everything rescheduled until after the trial."

"Thanks, Becca." She dropped the phone in the receiver and turned to see Tanner burping Lilly.

"Such a good girl," he cooed.

She couldn't help but smile. "Here, I'll feed her some cereal and peas."

"Peas?" Tanner wrinkled his nose. "Sounds disgusting."

"They're not disgusting—they're healthy." She took Lilly from him and strapped her into the car seat sitting atop her desk. She tied a bib around Lilly's neck, more to protect her suit jacket and blouse than the baby.

As she fed Lilly she heard Tanner's phone ring.

"Hey, Colt." There was a pause before Tanner responded, "It's no problem. I appreciate you checking the place out. We're fine here until you return."

"He found something?" She met Tanner's gaze.

"Yeah, a small house. He's checking it out now and may be a little late with the food."

She was about to ask which city, but Tanner shook his head. She nodded, understanding they weren't going to discuss the safe-house location until they were outside in the SUV, far away from Cheyenne and the courthouse. "Poor Colt, I'm sure he's frustrated with running late for lunch."

Tanner chuckled. "He'll survive."

"I know." Her own smile faded as she thought of the lengths these men were going to keep her and Lilly safe.

She hoped it would be enough.

Tanner packed Lilly's toys, thinking about the safe house Colt was checking out for them. As promised, Colt hadn't mentioned any details, but Tanner had wanted him to check out the place for himself, prior to taking Sidney and Lilly there.

That Colt was willing to postpone his lunch was an indication he took his responsibility of vetting a new safe house seriously. He was blessed to have good friends like Colt and Slade.

His gaze was drawn to where Sidney was feeding Lilly. Despite the disgusting green color, Lilly was eating the mashed peas without a problem. Remembering the red scar on the baby's chest, he could understand the importance of the baby having good nutrition. He shook his head, wondering how any parent could walk away from adopting a baby over a child having health issues.

Children were a gift from God. It pained him to think about how he'd lost Emily and the family he'd always wanted.

Some marshals were able to make relationships work, despite the travel and the erratic hours. But many relationships disintegrated under the weight of prolonged absences. His being at a safe house for the next three days with Sidney was proof of that. A woman wanted her husband home, protecting her and her children, not out protecting random strangers.

He thought about how Slade Brooks had transferred to a different position in order to make his upcoming marriage to Robyn Lowry work. Tanner liked his job, liked the variety of tasks he was presented with.

Was he willing to give it all up for a woman? Until now, his response was a resounding no.

But watching Sidney with Lilly made him second-guess his career choice.

Then again, if he hadn't chosen to work for the US Marshals, he wouldn't be here in Judge Logan's chambers right now, protecting her and her daughter.

A knock at the door from the hallway interrupted his chaotic thoughts. He glanced at Sidney. "Expecting anyone?"

"No." She'd finished feeding Lilly and was using a wet wipe to wash the green peas from the baby's hands and face. She set the baby on the floor next to her building blocks. "But I'm sure it's just Becca, or another court employee with a question."

"Yeah, probably." Tanner approached the door. There wasn't a peephole, like some motels or apartments had. Still, they were in a secure courtroom, so he didn't expect anyone to come rushing through the door, guns blazing. And he knew Becca often came into the judge's chambers, although she generally used the door from the courtroom, not the one from the hallway.

When he opened the door, no one was there. His gaze dropped to the floor. He frowned at the box of flowers.

All his instincts went on full alert. He slammed the door, locked it and turned to scoop Lilly off the floor. "Into the bathroom, now! Hurry!"

"What's going on?" Sidney looked confused.

"Who would send you flowers?" Tanner demanded as they crowded into the bathroom. He closed the door and locked it.

"No one," she admitted fearfully.

That was exactly what he'd thought. "Get down." Keeping his back to the door, he thrust Lilly into her arms, then placed himself between the woman and the child, and the door. A second later, a loud explosion rocked the room.

It confirmed what Tanner had suspected. The flowers were camouflage for something dangerous.

Like a bomb.

SIX

As the explosion rocked around her, Sidney curled her body around Lilly, sandwiching the little girl between herself and Tanner. Prayers she hadn't uttered in years, she reverently whispered now.

Please, Lord, keep us all safe in Your care!

The silence following the explosion was nearly as painful as the ear-splitting sound. The courthouse was never this quiet. Then she heard a frenzied knocking at the door leading from her chambers to the courtroom.

"Judge Logan? Judge Logan, are you okay?" Becca's voice was frantic. Sidney lifted her head to look at Tanner, who looked grim.

"Are you hurt?" He gazed at her with concern.

"No. Thanks to you, we're fine." She glanced down at the crying baby.

"Stay here while I investigate." He eased back and rose.

"Wait." She staggered to her feet. "I need to come with you. That bomb was meant for me."

Tanner hesitated, then nodded. The knocking continued, as Becca called to her. "Is the door between us and the courtroom locked?" he asked.

"Yes." She swallowed hard. "Ever since Santiago insisted on attending each of his hearings, I've tried to remember to lock the door when I go in or out." At the time she'd considered her actions a bit paranoid.

Now she was glad she had.

"Smart move." A flash of approval crossed Tanner's blue eyes. "You'll want to keep doing that, once the trial gets underway."

The trial. The thought of moving forward made her feel sick to her stomach. She hitched Lilly in her arms and followed Tanner. The door between her chambers and the hallway was hanging open from the blast, and her paperwork was strewn everywhere. Thankfully she had the important information on the trial locked in her briefcase. As she crossed over, she found her briefcase on its side, but otherwise intact.

Several deputies were standing in the doorway, looking down at the blackened remains of what she assumed were the flowers Tanner mentioned. "What happened?" one of the deputies asked.

"Someone left flowers for the judge, but as you can see, it was really a bomb." Tanner pinned them with a stern look. "We need to see who delivered them, who signed for them and how they got through security."

For a moment, the deputies just looked at each other.

"Now!" Tanner barked. "Every federal courthouse has security cameras. I want to see the video ASAP."

"We'll get right on it." The older deputy nodded.

"Where's Deputy Kramer?" Sidney asked, glancing around in concern. "He's usually assigned to my courtroom."

"Here, Judge." Kramer appeared in the open doorway, accompanied by her clerk, Becca. "We were in the courtroom and couldn't get into your chambers. Are you okay?"

"We're fine, thanks." She glanced at Becca. "Do you know anything about the flowers?"

"Me?" Becca's voice came out in a squeak. "No! Why would I?"

Tanner moved forward, stepping carefully around the paperwork. "Becca, you're aware of the threats against Judge Logan, correct?"

Becca's eyes widened. "Yes, I'm aware. I've seen the notes. All correspondence to the judge comes to me first, before it gets passed on to her."

"Then how is it that you don't know anything about the flower delivery?"

Sidney caught a flash of something, maybe guilt, in Becca's gaze. "I...don't know."

"Are you sure about that?" Tanner pressed.

Becca's expression crumpled. "They were from the judge's ex-husband, Gary."

"No way." Sidney's denial was automatic. "There's no reason on earth for Gary to send me flowers."

"I signed for them, and the card indicated they were from Gary," Becca insisted. "I had no way of knowing there was something more inside!"

There was a note of desperation in Becca's voice that gave Sidney pause. The clerk knew she'd been wrong to accept the flowers, and even if she had, why had the box been left outside the doorway leading to the hallway, rather than the door between the courtroom and her chambers?

To neutralize the damage from the blast.

"Deputy Kramer? I need you to place Becca Rice in custody until further notice." Tanner grabbed the woman, who instinctively backed away. "You're not going anywhere, Ms. Rice. Not until we understand what exactly is going on."

"It was her ex-husband who sent the flowers," Becca repeated.

Tanner leaned in. "I don't care what the card said, you knew about the threats and brought the flowers up here, anyway, didn't you?"

Becca didn't answer.

"It's only a matter of time before I get the security video," Tanner went on. "And I'm sure the deputies downstairs manning the metal detector will remember you coming down for a delivery."

Becca lowered her face in her hands and began to sob. "I knew I shouldn't have brought them, but I thought they might cheer her up."

Sidney wasn't buying her act. Shifting Lilly, who had thankfully stopped crying, to her other hip, she approached the clerk. "Why in the world would you do this, Becca? Someone could have been seriously hurt or killed!"

"Do you understand what the prison term is for someone who attempts to murder a judge?" Tanner asked. "You're going away for a long time, Becca."

"No-o-o," she wailed. "I can't go to jail, I have a son. I'm all Jeff has! You can't do this to me!"

A son. Sidney met Tanner's gaze and blew out a breath. She understood now exactly what had happened.

"Did Santiago threaten your son, Becca?" Sidney tried to capture the clerk's gaze. "Is that why you went down to pick up the flowers?"

Becca winced and looked away. "Yes," she finally whispered. "I was told to pick up the flower delivery and bring it to you, or my son would die." Tears rolled down her cheeks. "I'm a single mother. Jeff is only nine years old and is vulnerable at school while I'm here at work. Don't you see? I couldn't risk anything happening to him."

"Oh, Becca." Sidney was torn between wanting to scream at the woman and hugging her tight. "You should have told us, especially Marshal Wilcox, about the threats."

"They said not to or else." Becca's voice had dropped so low it was difficult to hear. Then the clerk abruptly turned toward Sidney. "I'm not a judge like you," she spat. "My life is nothing compared to being a judge, right?"

"Wrong, Becca." Tanner tightened his grip on her arm, as if afraid the woman would launch herself at Sidney. "All federal court employees are offered protection, so there is no reason for you to have done this."

"My son…" Her voice trickled off.

Lilly wrapped a chubby fist in her hair, and as Sidney gazed down at her foster daughter, she could understand some of Becca's panic.

Threatening an innocent child was a terrible thing to do. Parents were vulnerable when it came to their children. Sidney wished Becca had chosen a different way to handle the threat, but she couldn't help feeling sorry for the single mom, too.

The real bad guy here was Santiago and his hired men, who would stop at nothing to get what they wanted.

Nothing.

"You said *they*," Tanner said, refusing to be moved by Becca's tears or her temper tantrum. "I need to know who *they* are."

Becca shrugged. "Two men caught me outside my apartment building. I don't know their names."

"Marshal?" Tanner glanced over to where

the sheriff's deputy stood in the doorway. "We have the video. It appears Becca Rice picked up the flower delivery downstairs and bypassed the metal detector to bring it up here."

It was exactly as Tanner had suspected, but he was still angry. "And why did the deputies allow her to bypass the metal detector?"

The deputy's face reddened. "They shouldn't have."

Yeah, no kidding. Tanner swallowed the urge to yell. "I want those deputies reported to your superior. And I want a copy of the video sent to me." He rattled off his email address. "And lastly, I want you to get the word out that no one is to bypass the metal detector again. Understand?"

"Yes, I can only apologize for the lapse, Marshal Wilcox." To his credit, the deputy knew they'd messed up, big-time.

It was a mistake that could have had horrific consequences.

What if Sidney had opened the door and brought the flowers into her chamber? The thought made his blood congeal.

It wasn't just Sidney's life on the line here, but Lilly's, too. What would happen to the baby if Sidney couldn't adopt her? No doubt she'd be sent back into the system.

Wrestling his anger under control, he turned to look at Becca. "Describe the two men."

Becca continued staring at the floor. "There was nothing very unique about them—they were just two men."

"Yeah, see, that's not going to work for me," Tanner said. "You either cooperate with us or suffer the consequences of being tossed in jail. Your choice."

Becca began to cry again, but Tanner ignored her tears. "You are an accomplice to the attempted murder of a judge, Ms. Rice. Now start talking."

The clerk managed to pull herself together. "One of the men was Hispanic, the other was white. Both had short dark hair and are roughly in their thirties."

"Identifying marks? Tattoos? Piercings?" Tanner prompted. The description she'd provided thus far was completely useless.

Becca swiped at her face. "The white guy had a tattoo along the side of his neck." Her voice hitched. "I—I think it was a knife or maybe a sword."

"And the other man? Surely there's something more you can remember about him."

Becca shook her head. "No tattoo that I remember. Maybe a stud earring, but that's all."

It wasn't nearly enough. "Would you recognize them from a photo array?"

"Yes." This time, she didn't hesitate. "I'm sure I could pick them out of a lineup."

He debated whether to have her work with a sketch artist, or simply provide mug shots for her to review.

"What in the world happened here?" Colt asked incredulously.

Tanner looked to see his buddy holding a large bag of Chinese food, standing near the blackened mess on the floor. "It's a long story. I'll fill you in on the details later, but as you can see, someone attempted to attack Sidney with a bomb."

Colt whistled between his teeth. "We need to get the judge out of here. And make sure that door is replaced and the doorjamb repaired before next Monday."

Tanner was definitely on board with that plan. He eyed the deputy at the door, who nodded. "We'll get everything fixed this afternoon."

"Thanks." That was the easy part. He also needed more information from Becca on the men who'd planned this. "Call Crane, would you? Ms. Rice and her son, Jeff, will need protection as they help identify the two men who'd arranged for the flower bomb."

Becca sniffled. "Thank you, Marshal."

He pinned her with a fierce gaze. "You made a huge mistake, Ms. Rice. It's up to you to rectify that by helping us to identify the two men who approached you. If we can identify them, and prove they're associates of Santiago, additional charges can be filed against the guy."

For the first time since entering the judge's chambers, Becca straightened and nodded. "Yes, you're right. I should have thought of that."

Yes, she should have. But then again, he could understand that having your child threatened could paralyze a single mother with fear.

It was the same fear he'd glimpsed in Sidney's eyes, when she talked about Lilly's safety.

"I'll do whatever you need, Marshal," Becca said. "As long as my son is safe." She paused, then added in a low voice, "I know it's more than I deserve."

"It's okay, Becca." Sidney stepped forward. "You're doing the right thing now. The marshals will keep you safe."

Tanner glanced at Colt, who nodded. "I'll make the call." He went in and set the Chinese food on Sidney's desk, then stepped back in the hallway.

Doing his best to ignore the tantalizing scents of soy sauce and garlic emanating from the bag, Tanner glanced at Sidney. "Do you have everything you need to leave?"

She shifted the baby to her other hip, then bent down to pick up the papers that were strewn about the floor. "In a minute."

"Here, I'll get them. Sit down," Tanner said. She looked exhausted and the day was barely half over.

Sidney smiled gratefully, then went over and dropped into the seat behind her desk. Lilly was babbling again, clearly over her initial fright from the loud explosion.

Tanner tried not to dwell on the close

call. All they could do was move forward from here.

In hindsight, he was glad he'd asked Colt to secure a new safe house for them. And even he didn't know the location yet.

There was no way he was going to allow that location to be leaked to Santiago's men.

When he finished gathering all the papers, he stood and placed them on Sidney's desk. Then he eyed Becca. Leak. From within the courthouse?

"When?" he demanded.

She looked confused. "When what?"

"When did the two men approach you? I want the date and time."

She looked away, verifying his suspicions. "A couple of days ago in the morning."

"Days?" Sidney echoed in horror.

"It was you who leaked information about the judge's schedule with her nanny and the judge's location, wasn't it?"

Becca must have sensed he was on the

verge of losing his temper because she edged closer to the door. "Yes," she whispered.

"You caused Camella's murder!" Sidney leaped from her chair, startling her daughter, who cried out in alarm. "How could you?"

"I didn't know anyone was going to be murdered," Becca protested. "They only mentioned giving the nanny a message, not that they were going to kill her! But when I heard the news..." Her voice trailed off.

"Camella didn't deserve what happened to her," Sidney said harshly. "I can't even look at you."

"When I learned she was dead, I knew those men would do the same thing to my Jeff." Becca's tone pleaded for understanding.

Tanner sighed heavily. "If you had come to us right away, Camella would still be alive, and you and your son would be just as safe."

"How could I know that?" Becca asked defensively.

Tanner didn't have time to respond as Colt returned to the room.

"A marshal by the name of Ken Stone will be here in ten minutes, to take Ms. Rice and her son into protective custody. Ken is bringing a computer to provide photos of known associates of Santiago for Becca to review." Colt reached over to pick up the food. "Time for us to hit the road."

"Yeah." And not a moment too soon. Although traveling with a baby meant taking time to bundle up the kid and packing the diaper bag. Sidney took off her flats, pulled on her boots and shrugged into her coat, as he took the baby carrier, and the diaper bag. He caught her gaze. "Ready?"

"Yes." She eased past Becca, and gingerly stepped over the mess in the hallway, leaving Tanner and Colt to follow.

When they were in the elevator going down to the main floor, he glanced at her. "I know it won't be easy, but God is all about forgiving those who trespass against us."

Sidney held his gaze for a long moment. "I know I should forgive her. I even understand how frightened she must have been for her son. But seeing what those men did to Camella..." She shook her head helplessly. "It was awful, Tanner. And so unnecessary."

"I know. But if Becca picks out the two men involved, we'll be one step closer to putting Santiago behind bars for the rest of his life. So let's think positive."

She summoned a smile. "Okay, I'll try."

"That's all I can ask." Tanner found it difficult to forgive Becca, too, but it was better to stay focused on finding the men who'd sent the flower bomb.

Before they struck again.

SEVEN

Sandwiched between Tanner and Colt, Sidney felt safe as they rode the elevator to the main level. Although she was still unnerved by the explosion outside her chambers.

And the fact that her assigned clerk had been responsible. If anything had happened to Lilly...

She shook her head, telling herself not to go there. They were safe and unharmed. Dwelling on the near miss wasn't healthy. And wouldn't change the fact that Becca had acted out of fear of her son's safety. Without giving Sidney or the US Marshals the benefit of the doubt.

Tanner's comment about forgiveness had surprised her. And had made her ashamed of her spurt of anger. It was humbling to think of Tanner putting his faith in God.

And somewhat ironic that she'd prayed for the first time in years as the explosion echoed around them.

"This way," Colt said, leading the way through the front door of the courthouse, toward the parking lot where their SUVs waited. She shivered as the cold breeze off the mountains struck her face.

"We'll keep you safe." Tanner's tone was reassuring.

"I know. But it feels like the temperature dropped twenty degrees since we came in this morning."

"It has." Colt frowned. "I'm sure our Chinese food will be cold by the time we get to enjoy it."

"We can always reheat the food in a microwave," Tanner pointed out. "Assuming the place you've arranged for us has one."

"It does. Hang on a minute." Colt held up a hand, stopping them in their tracks, then bent down to take something from beneath Tanner's SUV. "Alarm system," he said by way of explanation. "Ensures that no one can mess with the vehicles when we're not looking."

Like planting a car bomb. Sidney swallowed hard, realizing she hadn't even thought of that. Then Colt moved on to remove the same alarm from his SUV.

"They are handy little buggers." Tanner helped secure the infant seat, then stored her briefcase. "We'll follow you, Colt."

"Try to keep up," Colt joked as he slid behind the wheel of his vehicle.

Tanner simply shook his head. When she was seated, he backed out of the parking spot and turned to follow Colt.

"Any idea where we're going?"

He glanced at her. "I told you, a small house."

"I mean where, here in Cheyenne? Or in another city?"

"Not sure." The corner of his mouth

lifted in a half smile. "You're used to being in charge, aren't you?"

"Well, yeah. It's my job to run the courtroom." She tried to relax against the seat. "Although I understand better now why you've insisted on secrecy. I still can't believe Becca leaked information to Santiago's men."

Tanner grasped her hand, keeping his eye on Colt's taillights two car lengths ahead of them. "I know, but her cooperation in identifying these men will help us keep Santiago behind bars."

"Yes, that helps." A flare of hope rose in her chest. If Santiago could be pinned with orchestrating Camella's murder, in addition to the murder he was already on trial for, he may take a plea deal and waive his right to a speedy trial. Camella didn't have any immediate family to oppose that decision.

And there was no denying she'd like nothing more than to avoid facing Santiago in the courtroom. Still, it wasn't like he was the first criminal to stand in front of her.

And he wouldn't be the last.

For the first time she questioned her decision to accept the nomination to become a federal judge. It had been her dream, ever since becoming a lawyer. Turning in her seat, she glanced at Lilly. The little girl yawned and blinked, as if being lulled to sleep by the motion of the car.

Never once had she considered her job to be so dangerous it would place her foster daughter in harm's way. As Tanner had mentioned before, plenty of cops, firefighters and other law-enforcement officials had families.

No reason to think she didn't deserve to have one.

As if sensing her troubled thoughts, Tanner gently squeezed her hand. She liked how his warm fingers cradled hers. "You okay?"

"Yes." She told herself to stop wallowing in self-pity. Her job was to impartially preside over the trial. And she was more determined than ever to see this thing through. "Looks like we're heading toward Laramie."

Tanner chuckled, the sound sending shivers of awareness down her spine. "Yes, we are. I figured by how long Colt was gone that the place would be in Laramie. It's not as if there are many other cities nearby that are large enough for us to hide in for the next few days."

She threw him an exasperated glance. "You could have told me you thought the place was in Laramie."

"Thinking isn't knowing."

She refrained from rolling her eyes. "I half expected you guys to set me up in some ghost town. There are plenty around to choose from."

Tanner chuckled again. "No, internet and phone access are a basic requirement." His smile faded. "I'm going to be going through the list of Santiago's known associates, too. See if I can identify the men who tried to gun us down at Red Feathers."

"They could be the same two men who accosted Becca."

"Exactly," Tanner agreed. "Although there's no telling how many men Santiago has on his payroll."

"Too many." Her brief excitement at the possibility of identifying Santiago's accomplices dimmed.

"Hey. We'll find them," Tanner assured her.

She admired his unwavering confidence. His strength and kindness instilled a sense of relief in her—she was fortunate to have his protection. "If anyone can, it's you, Tanner."

He flashed a grin. "Colt's a good deputy marshal, too. Don't let his obsession with food fool you."

Her stomach rumbled. "At the moment, I'm the one obsessed with food. I'm hungry. It may not have been the smartest idea to let Colt take the bag of Chinese takeout with him. What if he eats it all before we get to the safe house?"

Tanner's grin widened. "Then we'll make him get more, but I'm sure he bought enough to feed a small army. I promise he won't eat it all."

"I hope not." She glanced back at Lilly, who'd fallen asleep. Her little face was so sweet, so innocent, it made her heart fill with love.

And fear.

"Do you think I should call Lilly's social worker?"

"No." There was no hesitation in his voice. "If Santiago could get to Becca, then he could just as easily get to the social worker assigned to your case. Best to keep Lilly with us, where we can keep a close eye on her."

"Okay." It was what she wanted, as well, and it helped that he agreed.

"I do have a question," Tanner said, intruding on her thoughts.

"What?"

"Why would Santiago keep trying to scare you with threats? What's his end-game? Wouldn't postponing the trial just keep him in jail longer?"

"I've asked myself that same question." She shrugged. "I honestly don't know what he thinks he'll gain from this. The threats specifically said to find Santiago innocent, but that's not up to me. That's a decision for the jury."

"But you rule on the motions, right?"

"Yes, but think about it. If I ruled in favor of the defense every single time, without taking the law into consideration, the prosecutor could file an appeal, or ask for me to be removed from the case. Which again, only prolongs his incarceration."

"There must be something we're missing," Tanner mused. "Are there other witnesses who may also be in danger?"

"Yes, there are definitely witnesses the prosecutor intends to call, several who are eyewitnesses to the crime."

Tanner glanced at her. "Well, let's just hope the endgame isn't to stall long enough to threaten the witnesses into refusing to testify."

"I hope not." She shivered, not from the cold, but from the distinct possibility that Santiago might very well do something drastic.

Like silencing the witnesses permanently.

Tanner followed Colt off the interstate and into the city of Laramie. No one had followed them, but that hadn't stopped Colt from taking a circuitous route to the newly designated safe house.

When Colt finally pulled into a narrow driveway, Tanner eyed their temporary home. The two-car garage was nice, and the location of the ranch-style safe house was directly across from Washington Park.

Granted the weather was a bit cold for Lilly to be outside, on the baby swings, yet it was nice to have the pine trees sheltering their location.

Tanner waited until Colt got out of his SUV and unlocked the door, then he slid out from behind the wheel. Since Lilly was sleeping, he carefully unbuckled the car seat so as not to wake her.

"Need help?" Sidney asked softly.

"I've got her." After slinging the diaper bag over his shoulder, he carried Lilly inside. The place was warm and nicely decorated, several steps up from the two-star motel they'd stayed in the night before.

Although personally, he preferred the cabin in Red Feathers. Isolated and cozily nestled in the woods.

Not that that had prevented the bad guys from finding them. At least now they knew their compromised locations had been due to Becca's feeding them intel, not because they'd been followed.

"Take Lilly into the bedroom," Sidney whispered. "She should sleep for at least another hour or so."

He nodded and strode through the living room to find the master bedroom. This would be where Sidney would stay. She certainly deserved to have her own bathroom.

And he and Colt wouldn't be sleeping at the same time, anyway, so it would be wasted on them.

When he returned to the kitchen, he found Colt and Sidney unpacking the containers of Chinese food. "Colt, I can't believe you didn't break down to eat something along the way."

"I deserve a medal of honor, don't you think?" Colt offered a wan smile. "Trust me, I wanted to dive in, but it didn't feel right to help myself without sharing with the two of you." He winked at Sidney. "Especially the judge. I wouldn't want to be held in contempt."

"Ha, ha," Tanner said dryly. "Let's heat up the food."

It didn't take long for them to eat. Surprisingly, there were leftovers, which Sidney packed up and placed in the fridge.

When the table had been cleared, Tanner set about making a fresh pot of coffee from the groceries Colt had stocked for them earlier.

"I need your computer," he said to Colt as he filled his cup, then held the pot up to Sidney wordlessly. She nodded, so he poured her a cup, as well.

"I figured you'd want to scroll through Santiago's known associates," Colt said.

"Yeah, I do."

"Pour me some coffee, too, would you? I'll get the laptop." Colt headed back through the connecting door to the garage.

"You really think you'll be able to find those men?" Sidney dropped into a seat at the kitchen table beside him. "You're assuming they've been arrested in the past."

"I am, yes," he answered. "I'm hoping they've had at least minor arrests for drug possession at the very least. And there's also the possibility that some of these guys are still listed as associates, with pictures, even if they hadn't been in the system before now."

She nodded thoughtfully. "How are we going to know if Becca identifies the two men who threatened her son? Her marshal isn't going to call us directly, is he?"

"No, Sidney. All calls are going through our boss, James Crane," he explained. "That way both of our locations remain secret, even from each other."

Sidney's green eyes held relief. "I'm grateful for the extra precautions."

More than anything, he wanted to gather her into his arms and hold her close, but Colt chose that moment to return from the garage. "I did a quick visual sweep of the property," he explained. "The snow is undisturbed all around us, except, of course, for the driveway." He flashed a grin. "We should be able to notice if someone approaches."

"Thanks, Colt." He took the computer from his buddy's hands and booted it up.

Sidney stood and refilled her coffee mug. "While you guys are scouring for Santiago's associates, I'm going to get some reading of my own done before Lilly wakes up from her nap."

"Okay. Let us know if you need help with anything," Tanner said.

"I will." Sidney left the kitchen, coffee in one hand, briefcase in the other.

"You really like her, don't you?" Colt asked.

"Huh?" He felt his cheeks redden, and was frankly surprised by Colt's keen perception. "I admire her determination to do her job despite the constant threats."

"That is admirable," Colt agreed. "But that's not what I was talking about."

Tanner fidgeted in his seat. He didn't want to waste time talking about his personal feelings one way or the other. "We have work to do."

"Hey, I'm not judging you for...well, being sweet on the judge," Colt joked. But then his expression turned serious. "Be careful, buddy. Getting personally involved with the person you're assigned to protect can make it difficult to remain objective."

"I know." And truly, he could appreciate Colt's concern. They'd both watched Slade's feelings for Robyn blossom into love during the time their buddy had been assigned to protect her. Slade had found it difficult to put aside his personal feelings to focus on the case.

And now, spending time with Sidney and Lilly, Tanner had a new appreciation for what Slade had experienced.

"Tanner?"

"Yeah, don't worry," Tanner said quickly. "I'm fully aware of the need to remain professional."

Colt shot him a skeptical glance, but Tanner turned to focus on the computer.

"Do me a favor and call Crane, see if you can find out if Becca has identified anyone yet."

"It's barely been two hours since we left the courthouse," Colt protested. "Besides, Crane promised to keep me posted. Oh, and I passed along your concern about Santiago's lawyer, and Crane said he'll look into the guy's background. For now, let's see what we can find by reviewing mug shots."

Tanner had been hoping for Becca to narrow the field of potential candidates. He brought the face of the guy he'd seen into his mind and began scrolling through the list of known associates.

It was painstaking work, frustrating on many levels. Not least of all, the fact that there were so many guys, and some women, who were known associates of Manuel Santiago.

Too many.

At one point he heard the baby crying,

but Sidney must have quieted her down because the wailing didn't last long. As he went through photo after photo, he despaired of finding the man who'd sprung from the woods to shoot at them.

Was the guy some sort of new player on Santiago's team? Someone Santiago's men had recruited to help hide the criminal mastermind's involvement in threatening a federal judge?

He hated to admit anything was possible.

The next face that bloomed on the screen had him straightening in his seat. "I can't believe it."

"You found him?" Colt leaned closer to look at the photograph. "Oh, yeah, that's the guy who shot at us. Although I can't see much of his neck tattoo with him facing the front. Only on the side view."

"What's his name?" Sidney's voice had him turning around in surprise. She was still wearing her business suit, but looked very different from her usual judge-like self with the baby on her hip.

"His name is Calvin Franco." He gestured to the laptop. "Does he look familiar to you?"

She stared at the image for a long moment. "No, although I wish he did. He has a tattoo of a knife on his neck. He must be one of the men who threatened Becca's son."

"We'll find out very soon." He glanced at Colt. "Call Crane, let him know we've identified one of the shooters at the cabin in Red Feathers. Ask him to get Ken to show Becca this guy's photo in a six pack photo array, see if she can ID him, too. But have him cover the knife tattoo. I want her to recognize his face."

"Anything else?" Colt already has his phone out and was punching in a number.

"Yeah, tell Crane to issue a BOLO for the guy, ASAP. We need to get him in custody, see if he'll turn on Santiago." Tanner sat back with grim satisfaction. Now that they knew one of the men involved, maybe they'd get what they needed to put Santiago away, once and for all.

EIGHT

Sidney found it difficult to tear her gaze from Calvin Franco's photo on the laptop screen. She didn't want to imagine him killing Camella, but she suspected he had.

The knife tattoo was particularly disturbing. Especially since Camella's throat had been slit by a knife.

She slammed her mind against those horrible memories. Hopefully Tanner was right about Franco agreeing to testify against Santiago. As awful as it was to lose Camella, it was worse to think the men who'd killed her would get away with their brutal crime.

It still made her feel sick to know Camella had been targeted because of her.

Because Santiago wanted her to be frightened enough to sway the proceedings in his favor.

Never, she silently promised.

"What about the second guy?" Colt asked, when he'd finished discussing the suspect with their boss. "Find him yet?"

"No, but I didn't get a good look at his face, either." Tanner scowled at the screen. "I'll keep searching but we'll need Becca Rice to come through for us."

Sidney wanted to believe her former clerk would, but these days it was difficult to trust anyone.

Except Tanner. And Colt. But mostly Tanner.

She gave herself a mental shake and turned to the living room. With one hand, she spread out a blanket on the floor and created a play space for Lilly. The little girl was on the verge of trying to crawl, and she hoped she'd be able to watch her daughter reaching her next milestone.

Foster daughter, she silently corrected.

For a moment she gazed at Lilly, hoping the family court judge in charge of her final adoption wouldn't hold these recent events against her.

Not that she could totally blame him, if he did.

Drawing a deep breath, she told herself not to expect the worst. Her adoption court hearing was scheduled at the end of the month. By then, Santiago's trial would be finished.

"Sidney?" Tanner's voice pulled her back to the present.

"Yes?" She hadn't heard him come into the living room. She quickly stood. "Did you find something else?"

"No, but there is a bit of good news." Tanner's blue eyes searched hers. "Becca positively identified Calvin Franco as one of the two men who threatened her son."

A flicker of hope warmed her heart. "Really? That's great."

"Yeah." He offered a crooked smile.

"Now we just need the locals to find and arrest him."

"They will." She had faith in the local law enforcement. Although thinking of the cops made her frown. "I never did give my statement about how I found Camella."

"I talked to the detective involved earlier when you were in court," Tanner admitted. "He'll need to speak with you personally, but right now, your safety is more important. He's going to arrange to come and see you next week, after court is adjourned for the day."

"Okay, that works. Thanks." She appreciated Tanner going out of his way to help make the process easier for her. "So now what?"

He rubbed the back of his neck. "I'm going to keep looking through Santiago's known associates, and other criminals who've been arrested for drug trafficking. Of course, Colt is already planning dinner."

She laughed. "He's hilarious."

"Yeah." A hint of uncertainty darkened his eyes, but then it was gone. She didn't understand what may have knocked him off balance, other than not being able to identify the second gunman. "If you have any food allergies, or things you don't like, you may want to let him know. He's considering grilling burgers."

"I like burgers, but he's planning to grill outside?" She couldn't imagine anyone would do that in January.

"Apparently there's a natural gas grill on the back patio." Tanner shrugged. "I'm not going to argue with him. He's the chef, not me."

"Me, either." Lilly chose that moment to roll over, giving a wail as she rolled onto one of her blocks. Sidney bent over to move the blocks and rubbed the little girl's back. "Hush now, it's okay. You're fine."

Lilly waved her arms and legs as if frustrated with her limitations. Sidney gently guided the baby onto her stomach, smiling when Lilly pushed herself upright on her hands.

"She's getting strong," Tanner murmured.

"She's a fighter for sure." Sidney thought about those agonizing days the baby was in the hospital after her surgery. How helpless she'd felt, unable to do anything to make her foster daughter feel better.

"It's a comfort to know God's watching out for her," Tanner said.

She glanced up at him curiously. "You really believe that?"

"Yes, I do." He met her gaze head-on. "Faith in God's love and support is what got me through losing my girlfriend. Those were the darkest days of my life."

She was surprised that he'd admit something so personal to her. "I'm sorry for your loss."

He nodded. "I'd given Emily my heart, but she died while leaving me. It was a double blow, really, to lose not just her, but know she didn't love me anymore." He hesitated, then added, "And if she hadn't been so desperate to leave me, she might still be alive."

"Oh, Tanner." She reached out to grasp his arm. "That must have been so difficult, but you can't blame yourself for her decision to leave you."

"Yes, I eventually put that aside, but God helped me through the rest of it."

"I used to attend church, but then discovered my husband was cheating on me. Worse, he'd gotten his mistress pregnant." She shrugged. "Considering he told me he didn't want children, that was a bit of a shock."

"His failures aren't yours, Sidney." Tanner's gentle voice comforted her like a blanket. "He obviously pretended to follow God's word, instead of following His commandments. But again, his lies aren't yours."

She tipped her head, eyeing him curiously. "I don't think I've ever met a man who spoke so candidly about his faith in God."

"Well, now that's a shame." Tanner's Southern drawl made her smile. "I'm happy to discuss my faith journey anytime you're ready to hear it."

"Thank you, Tanner." She felt closer to him than she'd ever felt with Gary. Which was a problem, as she knew from this point on she would forever measure men up to Tanner, only to find them lacking.

But Tanner was too young for her and deserved children. Better for her to stop longing for something she couldn't have.

Lilly was all the family she needed.

Yet deep down, she couldn't deny that Lilly would benefit from having a father.

Someone just like Tanner.

"Sidney?" Tanner's voice was low and husky. She instinctively moved closer, was drawn to him even though she knew she shouldn't—couldn't—lose her heart to this man.

"Yes?"

"You look like you need a hug." He pulled her into his arms and she gladly wrapped her arms around his waist. Then he kissed her in a way she hadn't been held and kissed in what seemed like forever. She melted against him, enjoying every second of their embrace.

His kiss deepened, but then Colt's voice from the kitchen doused them like a bucket of cold water.

"Tanner? Do you have a minute?"

Tanner broke off their kiss, but continued looking deeply into her eyes as he hoarsely answered, "Yeah, coming."

"I…uh." She wasn't sure what to say. Thanking him seemed inappropriate, but his was the first kiss she'd experienced since getting rid of Gary, and she'd never felt more alive than when she'd been in Tanner's arms.

"We'll talk more later." Tanner's low voice washed over her.

"Okay." Was that really her voice sounding so breathless?

Tanner moved away, joining Colt in the kitchen. "What's up?"

She couldn't hear their discussion about the case, partially because her brain was still buzzing from the impact of Tanner's kiss. Even if she could have strung two coherent thoughts together, it was better to maintain her distance. She needed to stay focused. As a judge, she needed to remain impartial.

Something that was growing more and more difficult with each passing hour.

In her heart, she truly believed in the justice system. That every man and woman deserved the best possible defense to charges filed against them. It was a system that ensured innocent people weren't sent to jail unfairly.

Did other judges find it difficult to remain neutral when facing a career criminal such as Santiago?

Maybe, but all that mattered was that she continued to be fair as the proceedings moved forward.

When Lilly was ready for another bottle, she realized her can of formula was running low. Carrying it into the kitchen, she held it up for the guys. "I'll need a grocery-store run very soon."

"Oh, I already took care of that for you." Colt jumped up from his seat. "Tanner told me what brand of formula and cereal you preferred to use, so I bought more. I added a pack of diapers and some jars of baby food, too." Colt grinned. "Tanner mentioned Lilly enjoys peas."

"She does, thanks." She glanced over at Tanner. "I can't believe you knew exactly which brands to get."

Tanner shrugged, although his cheeks reddened with embarrassment. "I pay attention to details."

"Well, thank you, Tanner." She turned to Colt. "And to you, too."

Colt tipped his hat, but her gaze returned to Tanner, knowing this was his doing. First his kiss, and now this. She wasn't sure what to make of her growing feelings for him. Maybe there was something to Tanner's faith in God.

She was blessed to have Tanner as her protector. Not just for herself, but for Lilly.

And she'd dearly miss him once the Santiago trial was over.

Tanner found it difficult to concentrate after the impact of Sidney's kiss. The woman had knocked him sideways, and he wasn't sure how to straighten himself out.

He seriously needed to get over this attraction he felt toward the judge. She was way out of his league.

Yet despite how he'd initiated their embrace, she'd kissed him back. In a way that made him yearn for more.

He was guilty of doing exactly the same thing Slade had. Getting emotionally involved with the woman he was in charge of protecting.

His job was to keep Sidney and Lilly

safe. And maybe along the way, he could bring her back to her faith.

But that was it. Nothing more.

No kissing, even though it was all he could think about every time he watched her with Lilly. It was why he'd pulled her into his arms in the first place. And kissed her. The studious and proper judge became a giant marshmallow where her daughter was concerned.

He enjoyed the transformation, far more than he should have.

Enough. Tanner dragged his attention back to the computer screen. Becca Rice hadn't found the second man who'd threatened her son and he was afraid the guy might slip through their fingers if they didn't find a way to identify him.

Very soon.

He forced himself to focus on the computer screen, although he was keenly aware of Sidney making Lilly a bottle. Her wildflower scent was distracting, although he did his best.

Their ongoing safety depended on him identifying the second shooter.

Too bad he hadn't gotten a clear view of his face. Thinking back, Tanner couldn't even say for sure the guy had been Hispanic, although the fact that both he and Becca had identified the same man swayed him toward that conclusion.

He went back to Franco's rap sheet, looking again at the two arrests that were on file, both for drug dealing. They'd taken place two years ago, and Franco had done minimal time because the quantities weren't that significant.

There. He narrowed his gaze at the name of Franco's defense lawyer.

Quincy Andrews.

Well, now, wasn't that interesting? Same defense attorney representing Santiago. Because Franco had been working for Santiago, even two years ago?

Maybe.

"Sidney?"

She glanced at him over her shoulder as

she finished making Lilly's bottle. "Yes?" From the living room, Lilly began to cry in earnest, clearly hungry.

"Get the baby." He waved his hand. "When you have time, I'd like some information on Quincy Andrews."

She grimaced. "I don't know much. Excuse me." Sidney hurried from the room with the bottle. A few minutes later, she returned to sit across from him, holding Lilly on her lap so the little girl could drink.

"What brought this on?" Colt asked.

"Guess which defense attorney represented Calvin Franco in his drug busts?" Tanner tapped the screen. "Quincy Andrews. Makes you wonder if Santiago has the lawyer on retainer, using him for any arrests that may be linked to his illegal drug business."

Colt whistled under his breath. "Now that's a very interesting theory. Maybe Crane will come up with something on the guy."

"Really? You think that's more than a coincidence?" Sidney asked. "I mean, there are only so many criminal defense lawyers around here. It's not like Vegas, where there's a billboard advertising a lawyer posted every mile."

"While I agree that Wyoming is different than Vegas, it seems odd to me that a guy as flashy as Quincy Andrews would lower himself to represent Franco for a small-time offense." He hesitated, then added, "Unless he knew Franco was linked to Santiago, like a small cog in an otherwise large wheel of the illegal drug business."

"We need to find the second guy," Colt said. "If he also has a criminal record, and used the same defense lawyer, then we'll know for sure it's not just a coincidence."

"I'm trying." Tanner grimaced. "Too many of these guys have earrings. I'm hoping Becca will come through for us."

"Crane will call when he hears something," Colt assured him.

"I know." He turned back to the computer. He decided to run a search on cases with Quincy Andrews as defense counsel. A list of perps showed up, and it was no surprise many of the crimes were related to drugs.

But not all of them. He frowned and leaned forward. There were several armed-robbery defendants that used Quincy Andrews as their legal counsel.

Maybe his idea was far-fetched. Sidney could be right about the lack of qualified defense attorneys in Cheyenne. He was probably making a big deal out of nothing.

With a sense of defeat, Tanner pushed away from the table and stood. Continuing to look at mug shots wasn't getting him anywhere.

Normally, he didn't mind protection duty. But with Sidney being a target, he wanted to be out on the streets, searching for those involved.

Lilly finished her bottle, and sat in Sidney's lap, gazing around curiously. Colt headed over to the fridge to pull the hamburger out to make patties.

"It's early to eat," Tanner protested.

"For you, maybe," Colt countered.

"We ate a late lunch," Sidney reminded him.

Colt grinned. "Don't worry, I'm just getting everything ready for later."

Tanner locked gazes with Sidney, sharing a private smile at Colt's antics.

When Colt's cell phone rang, he lifted his greasy hands from the bowl of hamburger meat and leaned toward Tanner. "Grab that, will you?"

Tanner pulled the phone from his pocket, easily recognizing their boss's number. "Crane? It's Wilcox and Nelson. I have you on speaker."

"We have a problem," Crane said in a grim tone.

Tanner tensed. "What kind of problem?"

"Do you have the local news on?" Crane asked.

"No. Why? What's going on?"

"A fire broke out at a house in Cheyenne," Crane said. "The address is two-eleven Cahill Road."

Sidney gasped. "That's my house!"

"Yeah, I know," Crane admitted. "The local firefighters have been able to douse the flames, but the house is a total loss. I'm sorry, Judge."

Sidney's face was pale as she stared at the phone on the table. "Do they know what caused it?"

"The fire marshal is still investigating, but based on the strong scent of gasoline, they're already calling it arson."

"Santiago's men must have done this," Tanner said, wishing more than anything there was something he could do to lighten Sidney's burden. "He's the only one with an ax to grind against the judge. And Becca Rice may have said something to them, as the judge mentioned working from home this weekend."

"Technically, there are other criminals who have lost trials under Judge Logan," Crane argued. "But, yeah, the timing is suspicious for the culprit being one of Santiago's men."

"You need to put pressure on local law enforcement to find Calvin Franco." Tanner reached over to cover Sidney's hand with his. "We need him in custody ASAP."

"This latest event will add pressure, don't worry. Again, sorry to be the bearer of bad news, Judge."

As Tanner disconnected from the call, Sidney pulled her hand away and rose to her feet, cradling Lilly against her chest. Then she walked out, going into her bedroom and closing the door firmly behind her.

Tanner scrubbed his hands over his face. Every time they took one step forward, like identifying Franco, they were hit with even more devastating news.

When would it end?

NINE

Her house and all her belongings were gone. Sidney found it difficult to wrap her mind around the fact that someone set her home on fire. Becca. She couldn't believe the woman she'd trusted for the past two years had helped Santiago's men.

And the worst thing of all was the potential impact on her ability to adopt Lilly.

As a foster parent, she'd had several visits from Tabitha, the social worker assigned to Lilly's case, to make sure Sidney had the nursery set up, and appropriate child care for while she was working.

At the moment, she didn't have either of those things. Not only would she have to find a new nanny, but she'd also need another place to live.

Overwhelmed with grief, she bowed her head and kissed Lilly, blinking back tears. If she lost this little girl now, because the state deemed her unfit to adopt, she wasn't sure what she'd do.

Start over with another foster child?

Everything inside her recoiled from that idea. Not that she wouldn't love to have another child, but she couldn't give up Lilly.

Not now. Not after having her for six months.

Not after giving the baby her heart.

She was so awash in grief she almost missed the soft knock at the door. "Sidney?" Tanner's low voice was muffled. "Are you all right?"

No, she wanted to scream. But she didn't. Instead, she gently set Lilly in the center of the bed, then kept a wary eye on her so she didn't roll off, as she crossed to the door. She wiped her eyes, then opened it.

"I—I'd like to be alone for a while." She

couldn't bring herself to meet his compassionate gaze. Pity wasn't going to help her keep Lilly.

And she honestly wasn't sure what would.

"Sidney, we'll find a way to get your house rebuilt. The insurance…" He hesitated, then asked, "You do have homeowner's insurance, right?"

"Yes, but that's not the issue. I know the place will eventually be either leveled or repaired." She glanced over at Lilly, who had grabbed her feet with her hands. "I'm more afraid the fire will hurt my ability to adopt Lilly. The state has strict rules for foster parents, including a bedroom for the child."

"I'm sure we'll be able to find temporary housing for you, complete with extra bedrooms." Tanner edged closer and she finally met his gaze. "I'll help you through this, Sidney."

"Thanks, Tanner, but once the Santiago trial is over, I'm sure you'll be reassigned somewhere else." Needing distance, she moved closer to the bed, so she could watch Lilly.

"I have plenty of vacation time coming." Tanner followed her into the room, but took up residence on the other side of the bed, as if knowing her concerns about Lilly abruptly rolling off the edge. "We can even look for houses to rent in the meantime."

His earnest willingness to help brought ridiculous tears to the surface. Tanner's concern was so different than what she was used to, she wasn't sure what to make of it.

Of him.

Other than she liked him, far more than was appropriate.

"Okay, that might help." She once again swiped at her face, and tried to smile. "It's a good idea, actually, to have a place rented and ready to go."

"Exactly." He smiled encouragingly. At that moment, Lilly rolled toward him, not just once, but twice. Something the baby had never done until now. Tanner chuckled, scooped her up and swung her around in a circle, making Lilly giggle and babble something incomprehensible. "Looks like this little lady is getting rambunctious."

"She's never rolled over twice like that." Bemused, Sidney went over to stand next to him. "Guess she's learning to go after what she wants."

Tanner's gaze locked on hers and held for several long seconds. It took a minute for Sidney to realize what she'd said.

Lilly wanted Tanner.

As Sidney did. It was disconcerting, to say the least.

"I, uh, guess I could start looking for a place to rent." Her cheeks grew warm and she tore her gaze from his with an effort. All this togetherness was making her wish for something she couldn't have. "I think it's better if Lilly plays on the floor now that she's a rolling maniac."

Tanner chuckled again as he carried Lilly into the living room. "Did you hear what your mommy called you? A rolling maniac? Let's see if you can do that trick again, shall we?"

The way Tanner interacted with Lilly made her heart turn into a pile of goo. More proof that he'd be an amazing father to his own children.

Tanner set Lilly down, then glanced up at her. "See if she'll roll toward you, this time."

Sidney wasn't convinced, but she sat on the floor near the opposite edge of the blanket. "Hi, Lilly—come to Momma."

Lilly gazed up at Tanner, then back at Sidney. She babbled something again, then rolled over.

"That's a good girl, come to Momma," she encouraged.

Lilly rolled over again and then a third time, until she'd reached Sidney. With a laugh, Sidney picked up her daughter and beamed at Tanner. "Did you see that?"

"I did." Tanner's gentle smile filled her with something she didn't dare name.

"Hey, are you guys hungry yet?" Colt asked from the kitchen. "I'd like to get these burgers on the grill."

"Sure." Fifteen minutes ago, she couldn't have eaten a thin cracker, but now she was oddly famished. "Unless Tanner wants to hold off for a bit."

"Go ahead and grill the burgers," Tanner called, his gaze lingering on her. "We'll set the table."

Shifting Lilly in her arms, she pushed up to her feet. In a nanosecond Tanner was there, offering his hand. She took it, and managed a husky "Thanks."

"I'll bring the blanket into the kitchen. She may want to roll around some more." He gathered it up, along with several of her rattles. "I'll keep her busy while you search for a place to rent."

"After I set the table," she reminded him.

Tanner played with Lilly as Sidney

pulled out the dishes, silverware and glasses. Taking a seat behind the computer, she pulled up a list of rental properties in the Cheyenne area.

Thankfully, there were several to pick from, although a few were outside her budget. But she found two possibilities.

"Tanner? What do you think of these?" She gestured to the screen.

He walked over to stand behind her, and leaned forward to review the two properties. "They both look decent, although this one—" he indicated the second property "—looks like a better deal. Same price but larger lot with a fenced-in yard."

"That's the one I was leaning toward, too." She almost liked it better than what she had before. "I'll give them a call, see if I can put money down to hold it for me."

"Wait, I think it might be better if I do that for you." Tanner hesitated, then added, "I don't think having the property in your name is the best idea right now."

"I see." The thought was sobering. Losing her excitement over the find, she glanced over as Colt came inside with a plate of food covered in tin foil, shivering and stomping snow from his boots.

"Let's eat while they're hot."

Sidney closed the computer and moved it aside. Colt set the plate in the center of the table, next to the buns.

Once everyone was seated, Tanner bowed his head. "Lord, we thank You for this food we are about to eat. We are grateful for Your ongoing protection and we pray You continue to keep us safe. Amen."

"Amen," Colt said.

"Amen." The prayer came from her lips before she realized it.

She lifted her gaze. Tanner smiled encouragingly, making her flush.

It felt a bit surreal to be praying with

Tanner. As if she'd been jettisoned into an alternative universe.

One from which she had no desire to leave.

Tanner was thrilled Sidney had joined his prayer. He was so preoccupied with her that he ate Colt's burgers without tasting them.

After dinner, he arranged Sidney's rental property. It had never occurred to him that her ability to adopt Lilly might be compromised by her house being torched.

The cops really needed to find Calvin Franco, and fast. They desperately needed leverage against Santiago, something they could use to put an end to these ongoing threats.

The rest of the evening passed uneventfully. When Sidney and Lilly went to bed, he glanced at Colt. "First watch or second?"

"We're both exhausted, but I think I've

had more sleep than you," Colt said. "I'll take the first watch. Get some sleep."

"Okay." There was no denying he wasn't at his best. Tanner fell into bed, but memories of Sidney's kiss made it difficult for him to sleep.

When Colt woke him at three in the morning, he felt refreshed and a bit guilty. "Why did you let me sleep so long?"

"Figured you needed it." Colt yawned widely. "And it's been really quiet."

"That's good news." Tanner rolled from the bed and padded to the bathroom. Fifteen minutes later, he was in the kitchen making a pot of coffee.

His thoughts returned to the case against Santiago. He decided to keep going through the mug shots, doing his best to find other criminals who'd used Quincy Andrews as their defense counsel.

He didn't trust the slick lawyer farther than he could throw him, and truly believed the guy was on retainer with Santiago's drug crew.

He had a list of three names when he heard Lilly cry. In an attempt to help Colt get the sleep he deserved, Tanner went over to the kitchen counter and began to make a bowl of rice cereal mixed with formula. When a sleep-tousled Sidney came in with Lilly on her hip, he handed the bowl to her. "I have this ready to go. Colt is still sleeping."

"Thanks, Tanner. Will you get the car seat for me?"

He hastened to place it on the table so she could feed Lilly her cereal. The little girl stopped fussing, opening her mouth for the cereal like a baby bird.

Tearing his gaze from the adorable mother and daughter, he went back to searching for more clients of Quincy Andrews.

"What are you doing?" Sidney opened a jar of baby food, alternating the peaches with the cereal.

"Making a list of criminals who used Quincy Andrews as their defense attorney." He glanced up from his computer. "There's one guy here, Alonzo Cruz, who has an earring and used Andrews as his attorney." He turned the screen so she could see the guy's face. "I think he may be Franco's accomplice."

She stared at the man's image for a long moment. "Becca should be able to ID him, right?"

"Yeah, I'm sending the mug shot to my boss. He'll see that it gets passed on to her."

Sidney nodded. "I'm afraid I have to return to the courthouse this morning."

He tensed. "That's a risk I'd rather not take."

"My new clerk has an updated witness list that I need to review before Monday."

He turned to face her, watching in amazement how she could feed Lilly while carrying on a conversation about her work. "Who is your new clerk?"

"Bruce Matthews." She shrugged. "He

fills in when Becca is off, so I know a little about him."

He didn't know the guy and wasn't keen on letting Sidney get anywhere near the courthouse. "Can't he just email it?"

"I thought of that," Sidney admitted. "But I wasn't sure if doing so would leave an electronic trail to the safe house. And I hate the thought of the witness names being out on the internet."

Blowing out a frustrated breath, Tanner couldn't deny that emails could easily be tracked to a specific computer. Yet he doubted Santiago or his men had that that level of technical ability.

But Quincy Andrews might.

Again, he wouldn't put anything past the guy. "Is it that important to you?"

"It's something I do with every trial." She hesitated, then added, "I guess we could stop in on Saturday if you think that's better."

"Not really." He'd rather not go at all. Yet he didn't want her to put her job of presiding over the trial at risk, either. "Okay, we'll take a drive into Cheyenne, but not until Colt wakes up."

"Thank you." She finished feeding Lilly, then settled down to give the baby a bottle. "I'm surprised Colt's stomach hasn't led him into the kitchen by now."

"He let me sleep longer than he should have." Tanner quickly stood and crossed over to look into the fridge. "Looks like he bought eggs and veggies. I think I can manage to toss a few omelets together."

"Sounds good, thanks."

Tanner decided to make one for Colt, so that he could warm it up in the micro- wave when he woke up. After they ate, he cleaned up the kitchen, so Sidney could change Lilly.

"How long before we can leave?" Sid- ney asked when she returned. "I'd like to grab a change of clothes, too." Then she frowned. "Although I guess that means buying something at the store, since my house is nothing but a charred mess. I need a new suit for court on Monday and something comfortable to wear this weekend."

This trip to Cheyenne was getting more complicated by the minute. "We can stop and pick up some new clothes after we get the witness list from the courthouse."

"I appreciate that."

"We'll need to go out of our way to make sure we're not followed," he warned. "This won't be a quick and easy drive."

"I'll plan accordingly, with an extra bottle for Lilly."

He could only imagine what Colt would say. But if they were careful, they should be all right.

At least the courthouse leak had been plugged. Becca Rice wasn't giving any of Santiago's men the inside scoop on Sidney's whereabouts any longer.

It was a fact that lessened the risk, to a certain extent.

"Coffee. Food." Colt staggered into the kitchen at nine o'clock. Four hours of sleep wasn't bad, although Tanner had gotten a full seven hours.

"Here you go." Tanner filled Colt's coffee mug, then handed him the omelet. "You can warm it up in the microwave."

Colt did as he suggested, then dug into his meal with a satisfied sigh. "Thanks, buddy."

"Yeah, well, you won't thank me when you hear what is on our agenda for the day."

Colt groaned and finished his coffee. "Let's have it."

Tanner filled him in on Sidney's request for clothes and that she wanted to pick up the witness list from the courthouse.

"Okay, but we need to be sure we're not followed." Colt tapped his fingers thoughtfully. "I think you should go first, while I stay on your tail. And we need to get off the interstate and take a couple of back highways, which will likely double the time it will take to get to the courthouse."

"Agreed." Tanner refilled Colt's cup. "Thanks for not giving me a hard time about this."

"Hey, we're good. We can do this."

Tanner nodded, grateful to have Colt watching his back.

By the time they were ready to go, it was just after eight o'clock. The ride into Cheyenne was normally just under an hour, but their circuitous route meant that it took them double that time.

Tanner parked as close to the front door as possible, scanning the area before letting Sidney out of the passenger seat. Colt pulled up beside him, and subtly placed the two alarm devices on their respective SUVs just in case.

He protected Sidney's back as she lifted Lilly out of the car seat. He followed Sidney as she carried Lilly inside. Colt hurried ahead to open the door.

The deputies eyed Tanner's badge with identical frowns as they searched the pink diaper bag and escorted the trio and baby through the metal detector. Tanner knew these were likely the same deputies who'd gotten in trouble for allowing the flower delivery through. He met their gazes head-on, unwilling to cut them any slack for their security breach.

It was difficult to believe the bomb had only gone off yesterday. It seemed like eons ago. And, in his opinion, the deputies involved were fortunate they still had their jobs.

The three of them crowded into the elevator. "Do you need to go into your chambers, too?" Tanner asked.

"No need—we can go straight into the courtroom. It's not like we'll be spending much time here."

"Okay, but I'd like Colt to go in first."

She frowned, but didn't argue. Which was a good thing, because at this point, Tanner wasn't willing to risk her life in any way.

They walked down the hall, passing a handful of lawyers along the way. Tanner realized that even though Sidney's court had nothing scheduled, the other courtrooms were in use.

"Give me a few minutes," Colt said, before slipping into Sidney's courtroom.

Sidney shifted Lilly from one side to the other.

"You want me to carry her?" Tanner offered.

"No, it's okay." Her smile didn't reach her eyes. "I know this was a big inconvenience for you and Colt, but please know, I appreciate your help in getting the witness list."

"It's no problem. And we'll hit the clothing store as soon as we're finished here."

"Thanks. Hannah's Boutique isn't far, and it shouldn't take me long to pick up a few things."

Colt pushed open the door and gestured for them to come inside. "Your clerk, Bruce Matthews, has your witness list. But there's something else, too."

Tanner tensed. "Like what?"

Colt's expression was serious. "Another threat."

They approached the area of the courtroom where the clerk was sitting. Bruce was a little older than Becca, maybe in his early forties, with salt-and-pepper hair. He handed the witness list to Sidney. "Here you go, Your Honor. This is the updated witness list from the prosecutor."

"Please, call me Sidney." She took the sheet of paper with her free hand and glanced at it briefly, not surprised to see Becca Rice's name had been added. She handed it to Tanner. He folded it and tucked it away. "Thanks, Bruce."

"Your Honor?" A deputy stepped forward, holding out another slip of paper. "This was found on the floor of the courtroom when I came in this morning."

The deputy wasn't Paul Kramer. His name tag read Burrows. Tanner's gaze dropped to the note written in the same block letters as the others.

Find Manuel Santiago innocent or your child will die.

TEN

Sidney's blood ran cold when she saw the message that had been left for her. She cradled Lilly close to her chest and looked at Tanner. "He's directly threatened my daughter. What kind of monster threatens a baby? You were right. I shouldn't have come today."

"You're safe with us," Tanner said reassuringly, although she could see the hint of concern in his eyes. "We won't be here long."

She swallowed hard, thinking that in this case, not knowing of this recent note would have been better. Ignorance was bliss, at least when it came to vicious threats against an innocent child.

A wave of anger abruptly washed over

her, and she glanced sharply at the deputy, Archie Burrows. "You have no idea who left this? There are cameras everywhere. One of them must have picked up something. Why haven't you already figured out who is responsible?"

The deputy flushed. "We're working on that, Your Honor. Unfortunately, the camera for this floor wasn't working last night. We don't have any video of anyone slipping the note under the door."

"Isn't that convenient?" She wasn't able to keep the sarcasm from her tone. "How do I know one of you isn't working for Santiago's men?"

Both Bruce and Deputy Burrows looked shocked, as if she'd slapped them.

"Easy, Sid—Your Honor." Tanner placed a warm hand on her arm. "We'll take a look at the cameras that are available, especially those down in the lobby." He pinned the deputy with a glare, and the guy nodded in understanding. "We might catch a glimpse of one of the two suspects we believe are working for Santiago. If we find them, we'll have even more proof to use against the guy. Trust me, he won't get to you or your daughter."

It took effort for Sidney to control her anger and frustration. It wasn't like her to toss out wild accusations. But these were hardly normal times, either. Finding Camella dead was bad enough, followed by gunfire and a bomb outside her chambers. But this? She could barely see through the red wave of fury clouding her vision.

Lilly was innocent and would not be used by Santiago's men as a way to force Sidney into breaching her oath of office. She took a deep breath and tried to relax.

Deep down, she was relieved she hadn't called Lilly's social worker to hand the baby off to another foster parent. She had no doubt that Santiago's men would have found a way to get to Lilly even if she was with another foster family.

She only trusted Tanner to keep her daughter safe. No one else.

"Ready?" Tanner asked, still holding on to her arm.

"Yes, let's get out of here." She tried for a calm tone. "The sooner we finish our errands, the better."

"Let me know if there's anything you want me to do," Bruce said as she turned away.

She looked back at him. "I will, thanks. And I'm sorry for being upset with the two of you. This…has all been a bit much."

"Understandable, Your Honor." Bruce nodded, and Archie Burrows followed suit. She felt bad for snapping at them, and made a silent promise to do better next week.

She needed to believe the local cops would have Franco in custody by then, as well as his possible accomplice, the man Tanner had identified as Alonzo Cruz. Once Becca confirmed Cruz as the second man who'd threatened her son, the police could pick him up, as well.

Having both of Santiago's men in jail would change the dynamic of the trial. She found herself praying that Santiago would soon realize his attempt to assert his innocence was futile and accept some sort of plea deal, at least related to his initial murder charge.

It was a plan she intended to approach Darnell with, as soon as the two men were in custody.

"Sidney?" Tanner's voice broke into her thoughts and she realized she was standing in the elevator, staring off into the distance. Tanner was holding the door open, eyeing her with concern. "Ready?"

"Yes. Of course." She hiked Lilly higher in her arms and followed Tanner through the lobby. She frowned and slowed. "What about the video?"

"We already have it on a USB drive," Tanner said, gesturing at Colt, who smiled with grim satisfaction. "We'll have time to review it this weekend."

"Remind me never to make you mad, Judge," Colt drawled. "Those deputies were falling all over themselves to get us the video."

A reluctant smile tugged at the corners of her mouth. Normally she didn't make a big deal out of her position as a federal court justice. She wasn't into riding a power trip. However, it was times like this that made it nice to have the title and prestige to get what she wanted.

What she desperately *needed* was to stop these threats once and for all.

"Stay between us, Sidney." Tanner gestured for Colt to head outside first. Sidney followed, carrying Lilly, which left Tanner hovering behind her. It was incredibly humbling to realize these men had willingly placed their lives on the line for her and Lilly, doing whatever was necessary to keep them safe.

Tanner stayed so close, she could feel his breath on the back of her neck. He put a hand on her shoulder to halt her progress. "Give Colt a minute to check the SUVs."

She nodded, understanding these were extra steps they'd need to take from now on. Clearly, the marshals were not taking this most recent threat lightly.

And she wasn't, either.

When the SUVs were deemed safe and Colt had removed the tiny alarms, she buckled Lilly into the car seat. Sliding into the passenger seat, she glanced at Tanner.

"Do you know where Hannah's Boutique is?"

He nodded. "Yes. Are you planning to take Lilly inside with you?"

I am now, she thought. "Yes, we'll all have to go, won't we? I buy most of my clothes there, so I don't need to try anything on." She let out a sigh. "We should be in and out in less than fifteen minutes."

"Sounds like a plan." He hit a button on the console. "Colt? Hannah's is up ahead. You want to scope the place out first?"

"Consider it done," his buddy responded.

Tanner disconnected from the call. The way he swept his gaze around the area made her consider canceling the request to pick up a few things.

Would it be any better to come tomorrow? Probably not. She looked down at the pantsuit she'd slept in. Yes, her robes covered most of her clothing, but that wasn't the point.

She couldn't wear the same pantsuit and blouse for four days straight. No, at the very least she needed one fresh set of clothes for Monday. After that, she could get her current clothing dry-cleaned.

And the realization hit her again—this was all she had. The clothes on her back, her briefcase, computer and Lilly's diaper bag.

Everything else she owned was gone.

The ringing phone jarred her. "Hey, Colt," Tanner responded.

"All clear. Let's do this."

"Got it." He turned the steering wheel and pulled in behind Colt's SUV. Then he glanced at her. "Stay put for a minute."

"Okay." From this point forward she wouldn't argue a single safety measure Tanner and Colt wanted to take.

Tanner slid out from behind the wheel, then walked around to her side of the SUV. He opened her door, then covered her back as she took Lilly out of her car seat.

"You want me to carry her?" Tanner asked.

She didn't want to let Lilly go, but knew it was for the best. "Yes, please, once we're inside."

After they entered Hannah's Boutique, Tanner gently took Lilly from her arms. He and Colt stayed at her side as she quickly picked out replacement clothing.

"Will that be all, Judge Logan?" The store clerk, Ramona, knew her by name.

"Yes, thank you." She pulled out her credit card, but Tanner put a hand on her arm.

"We'll use cash," he said firmly.

Her first instinct was to argue, despite her recent promise not to do that very thing. She nodded, and Colt stepped forward to pay. It felt wrong for the marshals to pay for her clothing, but she told herself to get over it.

Once the insurance claim for her damaged house came through, she'd reimburse them.

Yet another thing she needed to worry about.

True to her word, the shopping trip didn't take long. Colt reached for the bag. "We'll be back in plenty of time for lunch."

A second later, the front window of the boutique shattered as gunfire echoed around them.

Ramona screamed.

"Down, get down." Tanner yanked her arm, pulling her to the floor.

She instinctively grabbed Lilly, clutching her close. Tanner and Colt both had their weapons drawn. "Get behind the counter," Tanner instructed. "And tell that woman to stop screaming."

She scuttled around the corner of the counter. With her free hand, she drew the woman down beside her. "It's okay, Ramona. We're fine. Tanner and Colt will keep us safe."

"I'm scared. I don't want to die," Ramona blubbered. Sobs had replaced her screaming. "Why is this happening?"

Because of me, Sidney thought guiltily. It was all because of her.

And Santiago's quest to be released from jail.

"Our SUVs are out front," Tanner said in a low, terse tone. "How do we get out of here with Sidney and Lilly without being shot?"

"I'm sure the local police are on their way." Colt's expression was equally grim. "I could go out first and drive around the back of the building."

Tanner had been about to make the same offer. But he also wanted to stay beside Sidney and Lilly, as he'd promised. "Okay, you'll need to grab my vehicle, though. It has Lilly's car seat in the back."

"I can do that."

Tanner tossed him the key fob. "Be careful. We don't know for sure where the shooter is located."

"Or how he knew we'd be here," Colt added.

Tanner had already considered that. Sidney had made the comment about Hannah's Boutique outside the court-room, while they'd waited for Colt to clear it. But he'd noticed the clerk knew her by name, and figured many of the staff within the courthouse would know she went there, too.

Another leak from inside the court-house? He wouldn't have thought so, but he didn't have an alternative explanation, either.

Colt crab-walked to the door, then reached up to open it. Tanner found him-self holding his breath. Thankfully, there was no additional gunfire.

Seconds later, Colt was in the SUV and driving away. Tanner let out a silent sigh.

Either the shooter hadn't wanted to kill Colt, or the guy had already taken off. Considering the shrill sound of police si-rens growing louder by the second, Tan-ner hoped and prayed for the latter.

"You okay back there?" He peered around the corner of the counter to where the women were huddled together.

The clerk was sobbing, but Sidney gave a curt nod. "We're fine, thanks."

He smiled reassuringly. "We'll be out of here soon."

"Okay."

"Wait." The clerk abruptly looked up in horror. "You're not leaving me here alone, are you?"

"No, ma'am," Tanner said. "The police are on their way."

"But..." She sniffled loudly. "What am I going to do? It's already freezing cold in here."

"Ramona, call your boss. Let her know what happened," Sidney said gently to the woman. "You'll be okay. I'm sure they'll replace the window very soon."

"I don't feel safe here," Ramona wailed. "Maybe I should go home."

"Do you live alone?" Tanner asked. The woman was not thinking very clearly.

"No, I meant *home* home. Where my parents live in Jasper."

"Talk to your boss," Sidney repeated. "I doubt the store will remain open after this. They'll close down for a few days until the window can be repaired."

The honk of a horn could be heard from the rear of the boutique. "That's our ride." Tanner touched Sidney's arm. "Are you ready?"

"Don't leave me," Ramona begged.

"The police are out front." Tanner knew he should stick around, but his first priority was to get Sidney and Lilly safe. He pulled out a business card and gave it to the clerk. "Give this to the detective in charge, and have him call my boss's number listed on here, okay?"

"US Marshal?" Ramona's eyes rounded as she looked at him. "You were the target? Not me?"

"Not you," he assured her, without correcting her assumption. He drew Sidney upright, grabbed the bag of clothes they'd purchased and hustled her through the back of the store. The sign above the doorway indicated the area was for employees only, but he didn't care.

Every building had two ways in and

out, as required by fire code. And they were going out this way, hopefully throwing the shooter off their trail.

"Poor woman is going to have nightmares for weeks," Sidney said in a whisper as he gingerly pushed open the door. He saw Colt behind the wheel and swept a gaze over the area, then pushed the door open wider.

"She'll be okay. Get into the back seat with Lilly," he instructed. "I'll sit up front with Colt."

With a nod, Sidney darted forward and slid inside the SUV. He shut the door behind her, then climbed in. Sidney was still getting Lilly buckled in as Colt drove away from the boutique.

"You'd better call Crane," Colt said as he navigated several small side streets in order to leave the neighborhood. "He needs to know about this."

"Got it." Tanner used the hands-free function to scroll to the number. "We'll need to have someone pick up your

SUV, too," he added. "Did you grab both alarms?" Colt nodded. It wasn't optimal to be down to one vehicle, but there wasn't another option at the moment.

Maybe on Monday they could arrange for Colt's SUV to be returned.

"What happened?" Crane asked in lieu of a greeting.

"We had a near miss at a clothing store about six blocks from the courthouse. Someone shot through the window. No one was hurt, but this happened on the heels of the judge receiving another threat."

"Another threat delivered to the courthouse?" Crane asked.

"Yes, sir." He turned in his seat to look at Sidney and Lilly. "A specific threat against the baby."

"Jerk," Crane muttered. "Why are you out and about, anyway?"

"It's complicated, sir." He evaded the question, not wanting his boss to know the details. "I can explain more later."

"The locals will want to talk to you, Wilcox."

"All communication needs to go through you, sir. I won't risk our safe-house location." He wasn't asking, he was telling his boss the way it was going to be.

No more leaks. Although he couldn't say for sure there was another leak in the courthouse. He imagined Sidney may have walked the six blocks between the courthouse and the boutique especially during nice weather. A fact dozens of people likely knew.

"Yeah, yeah," Crane groused. "I hear you."

"Any news from Becca Rice on Alonzo Cruz?"

"Not yet. I should be getting a check-in call from Ken Stone very soon. I'll let you know if the ID is a match."

Tanner tried not to let his frustration show. "The locals should have arrested Calvin Franco by now."

"I'm doing my best here." Crane's tone

grew testy. "I understand you and Nelson are in the trenches, but I'm handling other cases, too. I'll call the Cheyenne police chief as soon as I can to put some heat on them."

"Thanks. We'll be in touch later then." Tanner disconnected from the call.

"Nothing yet on Calvin Franco?" Colt asked.

"No. Just get us to the safe house, okay?" Tanner shifted again in his seat, so he could watch through the rear window.

After several moments, he noticed a black truck keeping pace with them. "Colt? How long has that black truck been behind us?"

Colt frowned. "Not sure."

"Well, you need to lose him." Tanner glanced briefly at Sidney. "Keep your head down, okay?"

She nodded and bent over in her seat, her hand resting on Lilly as if needing the contact with her daughter.

Tanner braced himself. Colt hit the

brakes and made a sharp right-hand turn down a gravel road.

The black truck followed them.

ELEVEN

Not again! Please, not again!

Sidney braced herself for the worst, fearing the occupants of the truck might start shooting.

Lord, I know I haven't been to church in a long time, but please spare my daughter. Please keep Lilly safe in Your care!

The SUV rocked and rolled as Colt increased his speed over the rough terrain. She didn't know where they were, but had faith in Colt and Tanner, trusting they would do everything in their power to keep her and Lilly safe.

"The truck is still behind us," Tanner warned.

The words had barely left his mouth when the sound of gunfire echoed around them.

"I've had enough of this nonsense," Tanner grumbled. She heard the sound of the car window going down. She glanced up enough to see him leaning out the window to return fire.

Lilly cried out at the loud sounds of Tanner's gunfire and Sidney couldn't blame her. She was scared out of her mind, too.

"Good aim, buddy, you hit one of their tires!" Colt's excited voice evoked a flash of hope.

They were going to escape!

"Keep going," Tanner advised.

She sat up, looking around while trying to soothe her daughter. "Shh, Lilly, it's okay. We're fine. See? We're safe now."

Tanner had his phone pressed to his ear. "Crane? There's a black Ford truck on Canterbury Drive, it's a gravel road off Highway two-ten, heading north. The occupants fired at us and I shot back, hitting their tire. I suspect those men are Calvin Franco and Alonzo Cruz. I need local law enforcement sent to this location ASAP."

Sidney couldn't hear Crane's response but knew the man was likely following up on Tanner's request. The bone-rattling ride continued for another fifteen minutes.

"I think you've lost them," Tanner said, breaking the silence. "Good work."

"Hey, you're the one who slowed them down," Colt pointed out with a grin. "That's some nice shooting."

"Yeah, God was watching over us big-time," Tanner replied. He turned to look at her. "You both okay? No one was hit?"

She managed a nod, her throat clogged with emotion. She felt certain Tanner was right, that God had watched over them.

How else could Tanner have shot out the truck's tires?

Yet somehow, Tanner had accomplished it.

"We're fine," she said hoarsely. "I don't think the SUV was hit, either."

Tanner nodded, his expression grim. "I wish I could have gone back there to arrest them."

"The police will do that, won't they?"

He shrugged. "If they get there in time. Plenty of places to hide out in the wilderness, even in January. Hunter's cabins, deer blinds, that kind of thing."

Her previous hope waned. "Let's hope they can be tracked through the snow then."

"Yeah, there is that." Tanner's gaze shifted to Lilly, who'd finally stopped crying. Her face was red and blotchy, though, and she was gnawing on her fist. "I'm sorry I scared her."

"It's okay, Tanner. She'll be fine." Sidney hesitated, then asked, "How long until we get back to the safe house? I may need to give her a bottle."

"We're going to be driving for a while yet, so do what you need with Lilly." Tanner's expression remained grim. "We're not returning to Laramie until I'm certain we haven't been followed."

"I understand." She was grateful for the extra care they were taking to protect her. "And I'm sorry, Tanner. I never should have insisted on getting the witness list and grabbing new clothes."

"Hey, if this little expedition results in the arrest of Franco and Cruz, it will have been well worth it." Tanner's smile was lopsided. "And we might get something good from the courthouse video, too. Don't beat yourself up over this."

Tears pricked at her eyes, a strange phenomenon that seemed to be happening more and more these days. "I'll try, but it's not easy. If Lilly had been hurt by that gunfire..." She couldn't finish.

"She wasn't, and it's not your fault, either. Santiago is likely the person responsible." Tanner paused, then added, "And we'll find a way to prove it."

"Thanks." She swiped at her face and pulled herself together. Tanner was right.

The more attempts these guys made to harm her and Lilly, the more likely they'd make a critical mistake, one that would result in them being caught.

Lilly began to cry again, still gnawing on her fist. Sidney pulled a bottle from the diaper bag and gave it to Lilly while keeping her in the car seat. It wasn't an ideal position, but she wasn't about to take the risk. Another vehicle could show up behind them again.

It seemed to her that Santiago had people willing to do his bidding far and wide. Likely thanks to his drug-trafficking network.

Disheartening, really, but she was determined to do her best to manage his trial in a professional and unbiased way.

Then a horrible thought hit her. "Tanner?"

"Yeah?" He turned in his seat to look at her.

"Do you think Santiago is doing this so he can get a new trial if he's found guilty?

Quincy Andrews could claim that I was biased against Santiago because of the threats."

"That's an angle I hadn't considered," Tanner admitted. "But it still doesn't make any sense to me. That could work against him, too, couldn't it? Say he's found innocent at trial. Couldn't the prosecutor prove you were biased against them and refile in an appeal?"

"Yes, ruining my reputation as a judge." Something that would likely end her career.

"Not to mention, he'd still be in jail, right? So what is he gaining by this?" Tanner shook his head. "Honestly, it doesn't make much sense."

"I know. It's a conundrum, for sure."

Tanner grinned. "I love when you talk like that."

She lifted an eyebrow. "Like what?"

"All judge-like. No one uses the word *conundrum* in regular conversation."

She scowled. "What are you talking about? Of course they do."

"No, just you, Sidney." Tanner chuckled.

"Stop teasing her," Colt said. "I need your help on which way to go from here."

Tanner winked and turned around to face forward. Sidney felt her cheeks flush with embarrassment.

Or maybe it was more of an awareness that made her blush. Tanner's smile warmed her heart in a way she hadn't experienced in a long time.

Too long.

Yet Sidney knew this was temporary. Being with Tanner, staying in a safe house, wasn't real life. Well, it was real, frighteningly so, but it wasn't indicative of her future. The trial would be over, and in all likelihood, she'd never see Tanner again.

Lilly was her future. Not a man, but a daughter.

A beautiful, sweet little girl who needed Sidney as much as she needed Lilly.

Allowing herself to become emotionally involved with Tanner was a sure path to heartache.

"Let's make a circle so that we're heading into Laramie from the west," Tanner suggested. "We should know by then if we've picked up another tail."

"Sounds good, but it will add an hour to our commute." Colt glanced at him. "Not complaining, mind you. Oh, and we should pick up something for lunch along the way."

"We're not stopping again, so figure out what you can make from the groceries you picked up yesterday." Tanner tried not to sound exasperated. "It's only noon."

"I can't help it if I'm hungry." Colt looked thoughtful. "I bought a couple of frozen pizzas, but we should save them for dinner. For lunch, I can grill chicken breasts. We still have hamburger buns left over."

"Whatever." Tanner rolled his eyes. "I don't care what we eat, just drive, okay? I'm fairly certain we won't starve."

"You mean, thanks to me, we won't starve," Colt corrected.

Lilly let out a loud burp. They all cracked up, needing to release some of the tension from the second near miss that day.

Tanner listened to Lilly's babbling and felt a sense of peace wash over him. That little girl and her beautiful mother deserved to be safe.

And deserved to be together forever. He wondered if Sidney needed support during her adoption hearing scheduled for later that month.

He wanted to be there, and celebrate with her during that momentous occasion. It made him smile just thinking about it.

But first, Sidney needed to get through the trial. He and Colt would keep her and

Lilly safe, while hoping and praying Santiago was found guilty for every single one of the crimes he'd committed.

His phone rang. Recognizing Crane's number, he quickly answered it, placing the call on speaker. "I hope you have good news, boss."

"The black truck was found empty, no sign of the occupants. They have a team out searching, but they're stretched thin at the moment."

"That's not good news." Tanner rubbed the back of his neck. "Anything else?"

"Don't worry, I saved the best for last." There was a hint of satisfaction in the guy's tone. "Heard from Ken Stone that Becca positively identified Alonzo Cruz as the second man who'd threatened her son. You nailed him, Wilcox. Good job in following the lead of these men all using the same defense attorney. Although I haven't found anything else on Quincy Andrews, other than he makes a lot of money defending guys like Santiago."

"I'm glad to hear Becca positively identified Cruz." Tanner glanced over at Colt, who grinned. "I assume you have a BOLO out for him, too?"

"Yeah, for all the good they're doing." Crane's tone turned cranky. "It shouldn't be this difficult for the locals to find these guys."

"Unless they have a leak inside the local cop shop," Tanner said. The idea had been niggling in the back of his mind, ever since they'd found out the camera hadn't been working on the floor where Sidney's courtroom was located. "I think we need to dig into the backgrounds of some of these deputies working the court-house rotation."

He heard Crane expel a long breath. "Just what we need, another leak," his boss muttered.

Tanner knew James Crane was thinking about the leak that had been found inside the federal marshals' office in downtown

Denver. That leak had almost cost Slade Brooks and his witness their lives.

It was no stretch of the imagination to realize the same scenario was playing out here in Wyoming.

With the local police as the source of the leak, rather than the marshals office.

"Call us the minute these two men are found and taken into custody," Tanner said, breaking the silence. "The sooner we can lean on them to turn evidence against Santiago, the better."

"Will do," Crane agreed. "Trust me, I want this situation contained as much as you do."

Tanner sincerely doubted that but didn't respond. He didn't need his boss to know just how much he cared about Sidney and Lilly.

It was his own fault that he'd allowed himself to become personally involved with the judge and her daughter. And there was no way to go back in time, to change his feelings.

Even if he wanted to.

Which he didn't.

"How much longer?" Sidney asked.

"A good thirty minutes—why?" Tanner glanced over his shoulder. "Do you need something?"

"Lilly needs to be changed." She looked around the back area of the SUV. "I don't think I can do that here."

As if on cue, Lilly started to cry. No doubt, from being uncomfortable.

Her crying went on and on. Tanner hesitated, then sighed. Thirty minutes was too long to keep the baby uncomfortable. "Okay, Colt, you win. Find a place to stop where you can get food, and Sidney can change the baby."

"All right," Colt said with satisfaction. "We're coming up on a small town now."

Using the word *town* was being generous, but there was a sub sandwich shop and a gas station/convenience store. Tanner slung the diaper bag over his shoulder and stayed behind Sidney as she carried Lilly inside toward the restrooms.

"Hold on," he cautioned. He pushed open the door and glanced around.

"You can't go in the ladies' room," she hissed.

"It's clear." He handed her the diaper bag. "I'll wait here for you."

Their stop didn't take long, and Lilly was back to her usual happy self once they were settled in the car. Colt was his usual happy self, too, since he had a large bag of sub sandwiches for their lunch.

From there, the trip to the safe house went faster than he'd expected. Colt pulled into the driveway, and Tanner got out to open the garage door. Colt parked inside, leaving Tanner to close the door.

Keeping the SUV in the garage was their best option to remain hidden. Tanner wasn't sure the black truck had been close enough to get the license plate, but he wasn't taking any assumptions.

He'd like a replacement SUV before Monday, but would deal with that later.

Colt pulled out the sandwiches and set them in the center of the table. "Dig in."

"I'd like to take a shower and change first, if that's okay." Sidney looked uncertain. "Would you keep an eye on Lilly for me?"

"Sure thing." He picked up the baby and swung her around. "Hey, pretty lady, want to dance?" He whirled her around and around, making her laugh.

"I guess we can wait to eat," Colt said glumly.

Thirty minutes later, Sidney reappeared wearing the casual clothes they'd purchased at Hannah's Boutique. Tanner liked the way she appeared more relaxed and hoped that the rest of the weekend proved uneventful.

"Now can we eat?" Colt asked.

"You didn't have to wait for me," she protested, taking the seat next to him.

Lilly was on her blanket, playing with her toys.

"Yes, we did." Tanner stared at Colt. "Right?"

"Yeah, yeah." Colt eyed the sandwiches as if they might disappear without him getting a taste.

Tanner bowed his head. "Dear Lord, we thank You for this food we are about to eat. We also ask that You continue to guide us on Your chosen path. Amen."

"And we thank You for keeping Lilly safe. Amen," Sidney added.

Her contribution to his prayer filled him with joy.

"Amen," Colt said. He reached over to grab a sub. "Help yourself—there's extras just in case."

"In case of what?" Tanner asked, helping himself to a meatball sub. "An abrupt extinction of all sandwich shops in the state of Wyoming?"

"Hey, you never know," Colt said between bites.

"I heard your conversation with your boss," Sidney said, helping herself to a turkey club. "Sounds like Becca identified Alonzo Cruz. She really followed through on her promise to cooperate with the investigation."

"Yeah." Personally, Tanner felt it was the very least she could do. "I'm hoping they'll find Cruz and Franco somewhere not far from the black truck."

Sidney nodded. "I hope so, too."

"We'll convince them to turn on Santiago, you'll see." Tanner shook his head. "One thing about criminals, they always look out for themselves, over anyone else."

"Maybe." She looked doubtful, and he couldn't blame her. Santiago likely had already arranged for Camella's murder, a bombing, setting fire to Sidney's home and finding someone to shoot at them.

Even hard-core criminals might think twice about crossing the guy.

"Anyway, once Lilly goes down for her

nap, I need to review the updated witness list and review some case law that I think will be challenged during the trial."

He wished he could assure her there wouldn't be a trial. Ridiculous, since there would always be another trial. Maybe not with a defendant with Santiago's history, but he knew only too well there were plenty of bad guys waiting for their day in court. He cleared his throat. "I can watch Lilly for a while."

Her green eyes warmed. "Thanks for the offer, but there's plenty of time. As you said, we're not heading out on another errand anytime soon."

They finished the rest of their lunch in silence. When they finished, Sidney sprang up from her seat to clear the table.

He stood to help, when his phone rang again. Another call from his boss. He glanced at Colt and placed the phone in the center of the table. He hit the speaker button. "Hey, boss, did you find Franco and Cruz?"

"We found Franco," Crane informed them. "But he won't be testifying against Santiago."

"Why not?" He glanced over to where Sidney was obviously listening in. "We have to lean on him hard, boss."

"He's been murdered. Knife slash across his throat. Just like the judge's nanny."

The sobering news hit hard. He curled his fingers into a fist, realizing one of their hope of convincing Santiago to take a plea had been silenced.

Permanently.

TWELVE

The memory of finding Camella dead flashed in Sidney's mind and her knees went weak. She sank into the kitchen chair next to Tanner, clutching Lilly close.

Franco was dead. Likely murdered by his cohort in crime, Alonzo Cruz. Had Cruz also killed Camella? It was all so difficult to comprehend.

Why had the men turned against each other? Or was it possible they'd split up, and Franco had been murdered by someone else working for Santiago?

Someone who knew the police were trying to find both men?

"Where was Franco found?" Tanner asked, breaking the long silence.

"In the woods, about a hundred yards

from where the black truck was located," Crane informed them. "One of the local cops stumbled across him."

"They're still searching for Alonzo Cruz, right?" Tanner pressed.

"Yes. At this point, the theory is that Cruz may have killed his partner, Franco."

Tanner grimaced. "I wonder if that's because the BOLO went out on Franco first. Maybe he was seen as a threat to Santiago's master plan."

"Maybe," Crane acknowledged. "Although I can't help but think you were right about there being a leak deep within the Cheyenne Police Department or within the sheriff's department."

She couldn't suppress a shiver. Tanner noticed and put a warm hand on her arm. "If there is, we'll know soon enough. In the meantime, we'll need federal resources to find Alonzo Cruz."

"I'm on it." Crane sounded weary. "I'll keep you posted on any new developments in the case."

"Thanks, boss." Tanner and Colt exchanged a look. "We'll do the same. Talk later." He disconnected from the call.

"Well, that's not good," Colt said, stating the obvious.

"Do you both think Cruz killed Franco?" Sidney could hardly believe she was sitting at the kitchen table discussing murder. "On Santiago's orders?"

"Either Cruz, or our leak within the local law enforcement," Tanner answered. He met her gaze. "These men were represented by Quincy Andrews. Is there any way to set up a meeting with him?"

"We can ask, but honestly, there isn't much he can tell us. His being their defense attorney is a matter of record, but he's bound by attorney-client privilege and would never tell us anything about what he'd discussed with Franco or Cruz."

"I don't like it," Tanner muttered. "How do we know Andrews isn't taking information from Santiago and passing it along to his other criminal clients? The law prevents a lawyer from partaking in criminal actions, right?"

"Yes, but we'd have to prove that Quincy Andrews did such a thing." She shrugged and shook her head. "Since his conversations with Santiago are protected that's not going to happen."

"Our best option is to get Cruz into police custody," Colt said.

"Yes, it's possible he'll agree to testify in return for a lighter sentence, especially since we'll have Becca's eyewitness account to validate what he did. However, be prepared that Cruz could just as easily call Andrews as his defense lawyer, who will in turn instruct him not to cooperate with us."

Colt scowled. "The law shouldn't protect criminal lawyers."

"I don't agree with that, Colt. Everyone has the right to a mount a defense against charges brought against them." She paused then added, "Even Santiago, and Cruz. The checks and balances in the justice system are important to protect against false imprisonment."

"Yeah, I know." Tanner sighed. "You make a valid point, Sidney. I believe in the justice system, too. Yet you have to admit there's still a possibility that Santiago's lawyer is breaking the law." When she opened her mouth to respond, he held up his hand. "I know, without proof, there's nothing we can do. Other than hope and pray the jury puts Santiago away for the crimes he's responsible for."

She nodded absently. Tanner's comment reminded her that she still needed to review the witness list. And make plans for Monday's trial. She suspected the voir dire process of narrowing down the pool of thirty-six people arriving on Monday to the twelve members and two alternates who would decide Santiago's fate would not go quickly.

Lilly squirmed in her arms, clearly impatient with being held. Sidney rose and set the baby down on the blanket Tanner had spread out.

The rest of the day passed slowly, the mood among them, somber. While Lilly napped, Sidney reviewed the witness list, then used her computer to research some of the case law she wanted to be familiar with prior to the trial.

Deep down, she'd secretly hoped there wouldn't be a trial. But it was clear that there would be. She worried about how to manage the trial while keeping Lilly safe.

Tanner came over to sit beside her. "You look sad."

"I'm okay." She glanced up at him. "I feel safe here for the weekend, but come Monday, we'll need a plan for Lilly."

"Colt and I have been tossing some ideas around about that," he acknowledged. "She'll be safe with us in your chambers during the day, but it's the nighttime that will be a challenge."

"I know." Just remembering how gunfire had shattered the window at Hannah's Boutique made her feel sick to her stomach.

"We'll find a safe place nearby," Tanner promised. "Don't stress about it."

"I'll try not to."

"I have a question about how the deputies are assigned to work your courtroom."

Tanner's question made her frown. "What do you mean?"

"Is it always the same deputy? I seem to recall back in early December, Deputy Paul Kramer was in your courtroom every day. As he was yesterday, when the flower bomb was delivered. But earlier today, Deputy Archie Burrows was there."

"The deputies generally stay with the same judge, but it's not a hard-and-fast rule. Deputies get sick or take vacation time, so other deputies step in."

"How often has Burrows been assigned to your courtroom?"

She had to think about that. "Not lately. The last time was back in October, when Paul took a week's vacation."

"Oh, he was assigned to your courtroom all week?"

"No, actually, he worked just the first couple of days, then another deputy stepped in." She held his gaze. "What are you thinking? That Archie Burrows is the leak within law enforcement?"

"Archie, or Paul," Tanner admitted. "Or it could even be someone else. The camera located on the third floor of the courthouse had to have been tampered with by someone who works within the courthouse."

"Did you review the video of the front entrance?"

"Yes, and we didn't find anything unusual. Certainly no sign of Cruz or Franco."

"I didn't think they'd show up at the courthouse." She shook her head. "I guess anything is possible, Tanner. But I can't go around accusing people, especially members of law enforcement, of being culpable in this crime."

He lifted his hands. "I'm not asking you to. I'm just trying to understand which deputies are assigned to your courtroom and why. I was hoping we could get one guy to be there for the entire trial."

"Or one woman," she corrected. "Not that we have very many female deputies."

"I'm not opposed to having a female deputy guarding you," Tanner protested defensively. "I just want a deputy we can trust."

"I know." It truly didn't seem like too much to ask. "I know Paul Kramer the best. Maybe he was just sick today. There might be a way to see if he'll be back by Monday."

"If you feel safe with him, I will." Tanner took her hand, and she found herself gripping it tightly. His blue eyes flashed with concern. "Something else bothering you?"

"Nothing." *Everything*. She swallowed the temptation to throw herself into his arms.

"Sidney." The way he said her name in his low, husky drawl made goose bumps raise on her arms. "I'm here for you, even if you just need to talk."

"I appreciate that." She couldn't remember Gary ever saying something so sweet. "It's just hard to concentrate on doing work while knowing Lilly has been threatened."

"I completely understand." Tanner smiled. "But it's our job as marshals to keep you and Lilly safe. Nothing you need to worry about."

She gripped his hand tightly. "I do feel safe with you, Tanner. And you're also the nicest guy I've ever met."

His cheeks reddened. "I find that hard to believe. Your husband must have been a nice guy when you first married him."

She wasn't so sure. "Looking back, I rushed into marriage with Gary. I had been focused on my career for so long, I suddenly realized I didn't want to be alone for the rest of my life. And Gary seemed to care about me, too." She glanced down at their clasped hands. "When I discovered he not only cheated on me, but that his mistress was pregnant, I was shocked." It was still embarrassing to realize how naive she'd been.

"Those are his failures, not yours, remember?"

"They are. But then he went out of his way to try and get as much money from me as possible." She ruefully shook her head. "Again, you'd think he'd be happy enough to move on. Why did he need to add insult to injury by suing for alimony?"

"I don't know, Sidney. Some people are angry at those who have more than them."

"Angry is a good description." She still felt bad at how Gary had accused her of being a mean-spirited shrew.

Tanner tugged her close and lowered his mouth to hers. His kiss took her by surprise, but she held on tightly, not wanting him to stop.

Tanner's kiss was everything Gary's wasn't. And it was a testament to how far gone she was, that she never wanted the kiss to end.

Tanner had known kissing Sidney was a bad idea, but he couldn't help himself. She'd looked so sad, so dejected, he'd wanted to cheer her up.

Lilly's crying broke the moment. With reluctance, he lifted his mouth from Sidney's and released her. "I'll get the baby."

"No, really, she's my responsibility." Sidney seemed off balance as she rose from the table and hurried out of the kitchen.

Tanner sat for a moment, willing his heart rate to return to normal, her wildflower scent making him dizzy. Sidney's kiss had knocked him for a loop, too. And this wasn't the time to lose his head over a woman.

Sidney's ex-husband was a jerk, but that only meant she'd be even more reluctant to get involved with another man.

With someone like him.

Yeah, okay, he needed to shove that idea right out of his head. Hadn't Emily leaving him taught him anything? He sprang upright and pulled out his phone to call Crane.

"What's wrong?" his boss answered.

"Nothing, but I want to arrange for Deputy Paul Kramer to be assigned to the judge's courtroom starting on Monday. Who can make that happen?"

"I'll take care of it," Crane assured him. "Don't scare me like that—I thought your safe house was breached."

"We're okay here. It's Monday and the rest of the trial I'm concerned about. Getting back to the courthouse, Paul Kramer wasn't there earlier today, but had been there yesterday. Can you find out about that?"

"I'll make a few calls and get back to you."

"Thanks." Tanner set down the phone and paced the length of the kitchen. His job often meant long hours of doing nothing but remaining on high alert for potential danger. Normally he didn't mind. Patience was one of his virtues.

But in this particular situation, with both Sidney and Lilly at the center of threatening notes, the inactivity ate at him. He wanted to do something to ensure their safety. Not just stand guard, but do the actual investigating to figure out the source of the leak within the local law-enforcement agencies.

And connect that leak to Santiago.

He went to find Colt, who was taking a nap. He didn't begrudge the guy some shut-eye. After all, Colt hadn't gotten nearly as much sleep as he had.

Backing out of Colt's room, he returned to the living room, where Sidney was playing with Lilly. He watched them from the doorway, smiling at the way Lilly giggled up at Sidney. Seeing them interact made him all the more determined to keep them safe from harm.

"Did I miss anything?" Colt asked, yawning widely as he came up behind Tanner.

He turned to face his buddy. "Not really. I called Crane, asked to have Deputy Paul Kramer on duty in Sidney's courtroom starting Monday morning."

"Because...why?" Colt looked confused.

"Because I don't trust the deputies. You saw that video. Deputies go in and out of the courthouse without even being checked through the scanner. We already know Becca and Sidney have been threatened. Why not a deputy, too?"

"Okay, that makes sense. I assume Sidney trusts Paul Kramer?"

"She does."

Colt yawned again. "I need coffee."

Tanner followed his buddy into the kitchen. "Let's poke into Archie Burrows's background. See if he has a family, or is in debt. Anything that would make him an easy mark to do Santiago's dirty work."

"We should do that same check on Paul Kramer, too," Colt said, filling the carafe with water. "Sidney trusted Becca and that didn't turn out so well."

"True." He opened up the laptop and typed in Paul Kramer's name. It felt good to be doing something productive.

When Colt had filled his mug with coffee, he quickly joined Tanner at the table. "Have you found out anything yet?"

"Using our resources through the federal databases, I learned Kramer has been divorced for five years and has no children." Both circumstances definitely had him leaning in favor of trusting the deputy. "No unpaid loans or late payments from what I see here, either."

"That's encouraging," Colt admitted. "Maybe we should check Burrows next?"

Tanner was already on it. When his phone rang, he tore his gaze from the computer. "It's Crane," he told Colt, then pressed the speaker button. "Boss? You have something for us?"

"Paul Kramer is in the hospital." Crane didn't beat around the bush. "Apparently, he's pretty sick. No way he'll be back to work on Monday."

The tiny hairs on the back of Tanner's neck lifted. "Sick from what, exactly?"

"I don't know—why does it matter?" Crane sounded testy. "Bottom line, he won't be assigned to Judge Logan's courtroom."

"It seems like a giant coincidence." Tanner locked eyes with Colt. "He was there the day of the flower-bomb delivery and now he's deathly ill in the hospital?"

"I never said deathly ill," Crane countered. "And I doubt the guy was poisoned or something." His boss paused, then asked, "Are you getting too emotionally involved, Wilcox? I can always send a different marshal in to take over."

"No, sir," he answered just a bit too quickly. "But I don't think it's paranoid to consider Paul Kramer may have been poisoned. Sid—er, Judge Logan told me she trusts Paul the most out of any of the deputies assigned to her courtroom."

"There are dozens of deputies on duty at the courthouse every day," Crane pointed out. "I don't think they're all working for Santiago."

"I know, sir." Tanner realized there was no point in pushing his theory. "We're checking in to the backgrounds of some of the other deputies on staff there, too."

"Waste of time," Crane argued. "Whatever they're planning isn't likely to happen right in the middle of court."

Tanner scowled at the phone. Colt lifted up a hand, indicating Tanner should back off. "Yes, about that, sir. We still need a safe house near the courthouse for Judge Logan to use once the trial starts."

"You don't want to keep using the one you're in now?" Crane asked.

Colt lifted an eyebrow. Tanner shook his head. "No, sir," Tanner said. "We believe the trip back and forth between Laramie and Cheyenne would set us up to be followed."

"Huh." Crane grunted, not exactly thrilled with the news. "I'll see what I can do."

"Thanks." Tanner tried not to let his dejected feelings about Paul Kramer's sudden illness come through in his tone. "No word yet on Alonzo Cruz?"

"Not yet, but you'll be the first to know once he's in custody."

"Okay. Thanks again." Tanner hit the end button on the phone. "Do you know of any way we can find out more about Paul Kramer's illness?"

Colt stroked his jaw. "I don't have any

contacts within the Cheyenne medical center, do you?"

"No." Tanner stared morosely at the computer. "Burrows is married, and has one child, a sixteen-year-old daughter. If Santiago threatened his family..."

"He's a cop. He knows full well there is witness protection available." Colt leaned closer. "What about his financial status? That may convince him to turn his back on his career."

"No debt." Tanner knew that debt didn't always matter. Some people could be bought, for the right price.

Even a cop.

"Did you say something about Paul being in the hospital?" Sidney came into the room with Lilly on her hip.

"Yeah. He's too sick to be on duty next week." Tanner rose and took the blanket from her hands, then stretched it out on the floor so Lilly could roll around without getting hurt.

"I'd like to call the hospital, check on him," Sidney said.

"I'm sorry, all calls are going through Crane to avoid anyone tracing them." Tanner looked at her. "Sounds like you two were close."

"Friends, nothing more," she assured him. "We were both divorced, and it was common ground between us. I'm sure he'd talk to me if I called to check on him."

Tanner looked at Colt, who shrugged. "A call to the hospital would be difficult to trace. They must get dozens of calls each hour."

"Okay, here." Tanner handed over his phone.

Sidney called the hospital and asked to be transferred to Paul Kramer's room. She put the call on speaker so they could all hear.

A tearful woman's voice answered. "Hello?"

"This is Sidney, I'm Paul's friend. I wanted to see how he was doing."

"You're too late. Paul's dead." The woman abruptly hung up.

All the blood drained from Sidney's face. Tanner stepped forward and eased her into a chair.

Whatever had caused Paul to be hospitalized had been serious enough to take his life.

Had the deputy died of natural causes? Or from foul play?

THIRTEEN

You're too late. Paul's dead.

The words reverberated through Sidney's mind as she struggled to absorb the impact. How was this possible? First Camella and now Paul?

Her stomach lurched. She pressed a hand to her abdomen, willing herself not to throw up.

"Can I get you something? A glass of water?"

Tanner's voice seemed to be coming from the other end of a long tunnel. Far, far away. Out of reach.

"Sidney, this isn't your fault." Tanner's voice was closer now, and she lifted her gaze to his. "We don't even know what he died from. Maybe he has heart issues or something."

Heart issues. She latched on to the phrase like a lifeline. "He did mention being on heart medication." She searched Tanner's blue eyes. "Do you really think he was admitted for a heart attack?"

"I don't know." She appreciated Tanner's honesty. "But we can't assume the worst, okay?" He paused then added, "Who answered the phone?"

"I think it was his ex-wife, Clarise." She lifted a shoulder. "His divorce wasn't quite as contentious as mine and he hadn't mentioned dating anyone." It was hard to grapple with the thought that he never would again.

"Okay, that makes sense." Tanner sat close, wrapping his arm around her shoulders. She gratefully leaned against him, soaking up his warmth.

"I wish we could find out for sure how and why Paul died."

"I can make some calls, but you know

the autopsy won't likely be done until Monday."

Autopsy. She lifted her head to look at him. "Do you think they'll do one? Or will they need permission from next of kin?"

"That's a good question. Based on the fact that he's not that old, I would think they'd do one."

"Per Wyoming state statutes, it's not a requirement to autopsy patients who are being treated in the hospital. Unless the physician doesn't know the cause of death, then they can request one. If Paul had heart problems, the physician may just assume he died of natural causes. Can your boss call and request one?"

"I'll check with Crane," Colt offered.

She'd almost forgotten Colt was there. Her senses were so tuned in to Tanner that she was oblivious to the second marshal, who was also risking his life for her. "Thanks, Colt."

Below, Lilly rolled into Sidney's chair

and began to cry. Tanner swiftly bent down and lifted up Lilly. "Hey, little lady, you're fine."

"She wanted to be near us, I guess." It made her happy that the little girl had learned how to roll to get from one place to the other.

"Bahahbah," Lilly gurgled and patted Tanner's cheeks.

"Right back at you, little lady," he said with a grin. The baby's antics helped lighten the mood. Sidney was still sad about Paul's death, but she decided to believe he'd died of heart problems, until proven otherwise.

"You're so good with her, Tanner." She couldn't help smiling at the picture they made. "You deserve to have a family of your own."

"Maybe someday," he said lightly. "My job isn't that conducive to family life."

She frowned, but Colt returned to the kitchen before she could say anything more.

"Crane has requested the autopsy as part of the case against Santiago," Colt said. "He's making the arrangements with the coroner's office now."

"That's good." Sidney let out a sigh of relief to know Paul's death would be investigated. Secretly, she prayed the findings would be that he'd died of natural causes, but if Santiago's men were responsible, she wanted to know that, too.

Maybe it was a good thing that the autopsy results wouldn't be ready quickly. Remaining impartial throughout Santiago's trial would be difficult enough, without adding that additional bit of information.

For a second, she feared she couldn't do it. That remaining impartial throughout Santiago's trial would be impossible.

Then she shook off the moment of indecision. It was too late. It wasn't like she could ask for another judge to take over the case at this late date, a few days before the trial. That delay would spin

Quincy Andrews into orbit. The attorney constantly reiterated that his client deserved a speedy trial.

Sidney silently vowed to find the strength and integrity to do her job.

She couldn't—wouldn't—allow Camella's murder to be in vain.

The rest of the day passed slowly. Colt grilled chicken breasts for dinner, adding lettuce and tomato to make tasty sandwiches. She fed Lilly peas and cereal for dinner. Lilly had peas all over her face and hair, to the point that Sidney had to give the baby a bath.

Which was okay, because Lilly loved playing in the water.

When finished, she carried a sweet-smelling Lilly back into the kitchen and stopped abruptly when she saw a stranger in the room.

Tanner quickly made the introductions. "Sidney, this is US Marshal Slade Brooks. Slade, this is Federal Judge Sidney Logan and her daughter, Lilly."

"Nice to meet you." Slade tipped his black cowboy hat.

"Same, but how did you know where to find us?"

"Crane sent me the information. Don't worry, I'm here to help."

She glanced at Tanner. "Do you really think I need three US Marshals guarding me? I don't want to pull anyone away from someone else in need."

The men exchanged a look. "We want to have two marshals in the courtroom with you, and one to keep an eye on Lilly."

This was obviously an added precaution related to Paul Kramer's untimely death.

"You'll watch Lilly?" She looked directly at Tanner. Then, realizing the other two may take her request the wrong way, she hastily added, "It's just she knows you and will be more comfortable with you."

"Yes. I'll stay in your chambers with Lilly while you're in the courtroom,"

Tanner confirmed. "And I trust Colt and Slade to watch over you when I'm not there."

She nodded, the band of tension around her heart easing a bit at his words.

"You can trust me and Colt to keep you safe, Judge Logan," Slade said. "Tanner and Colt helped keep my witness safe before Christmas, and I'm happy to return the favor."

"Please, call me Sidney." She already felt older than her thirty-six years. Having three young men surrounding her wasn't helping. "And I do trust you. I feel bad wasting resources, though."

"It's not a waste," Tanner said firmly. "You're a federal judge and it's our job to keep you safe."

Sidney nodded, although she suspected that Tanner had called in some favors to get the additional support.

It would be one thing if she was the only one at risk, but the most recent threat had targeted Lilly. An innocent six-month-old baby.

Favors or not, she was truly grateful for the added protection.

Later that night, Sidney watched her daughter sleep, unable to shut down her squirrel brain. Paul's death, Franco being murdered and the various case laws she'd reviewed earlier spun around and around in her head.

Close to midnight, she climbed out of bed and made her way to the kitchen, stopping abruptly when she found Tanner sitting at the table working on Colt's computer.

"Having trouble sleeping?" he asked.

"Yes." She went over to pour herself a glass of water from the tap. "Too much information swimming around in my brain."

"I'm sorry to hear that." His blue gaze was full of compassion.

She sipped her water. "I take it that you,

Colt and Slade are all going to alternate your sleep schedules?"

"Yes, and we will throughout the weekend and the trial." He hesitated, then added, "You'll never be alone, Sidney."

"To be honest, I never feel alone with you, Tanner. I mean, even with the others being here, you're the one that makes me feel safe."

His gaze warmed. "I'm glad to hear it."

The urge to throw herself into his arms was strong, as the memory of their recent kiss pushed aside all thoughts of danger and the trial.

She took one step toward him, then another. He rose as if to meet her halfway, but then Colt walked into the kitchen.

"Your turn to sleep," Colt said sleepily. Then he hesitated, as if sensing he'd interrupted something. "Unless you need a few minutes alone first?"

"No, of course not." Sidney flushed and turned away. "Good night."

"Good night, Sidney." Tanner's husky

voice echoed in her mind all the way down the hall to her room.

Tanner was relieved to have Slade on board with protecting Sidney. He didn't trust the local law enforcement, especially the deputies assigned to the courthouse.

Deep down, he wasn't convinced Paul Kramer's death was the result of a heart attack. Or any other natural cause.

Having Slade standing right beside the deputy assigned to Sidney's courtroom would give him peace of mind. Personally, he'd rather be in the courtroom, protecting her.

But he wouldn't go back on his promise to protect her baby.

"Anything I need to know?" Colt asked as he made a pot of coffee. Not only did the guy eat constantly, or so it seemed, but he also regularly downed a gallon of coffee.

"No. We're still waiting to hear something related to the BOLO on Alonzo Cruz."

"Okay, sounds good." Colt hesitated, then added, "Keep your mind in the game, Wilcox. Falling for the judge will only be a distraction."

"I know." He understood his buddy's concern—it was a lecture he'd given himself more than once. "Good night."

The next morning, Colt started making breakfast, while the rest of them gathered around the table.

"What's the game plan on a safe house?" Slade asked, helping himself to coffee. "Heard you want something close to the courthouse."

"One with a secret tunnel would be great, thanks," Tanner joked.

Sidney fed Lilly applesauce and rice cereal, smiling a bit as she listened to the conversation. "With the three of you guarding me, I'll be fine."

"I worked on that last night," Colt said, glancing over his shoulder. He was cooking bacon and eggs for the group. "There's a new home available for rent. It's furnished and located a half mile from the courthouse."

"That sounds like a good possibility." Tanner turned the computer to review Colt's latest search. "I like that it sits on three acres. Plenty of open space to see anyone coming."

"Yeah, my only concern was, of course, easy sightlines with a rifle."

Sidney paled. "A rifle?"

"Hey, didn't mean to worry you," Colt hastily amended. "I'd rather have open space around us than wooded terrain that could hide a bad guy approaching the place."

"We'll take precautions, Sidney." Tanner knew she'd balk, but he planned on having her wear a bullet-resistant vest. In fact, he was making a list of requirements for Crane. Although now that they had Slade's vehicle, he could scratch a replacement SUV off the list. "Do we need to let Crane know about this place?"

"Yeah, he should be the one to make the arrangements." Colt turned back to the stove.

"Make the call after breakfast," Slade suggested.

"Will do." Tanner eyed Slade. "How are things going between our boss and your fiancée's mother?"

"Crane takes Lucille out as often as he can," Slade acknowledged with a grin. "They say they're taking things slow, because Lucille's divorce hasn't been finalized yet. But it's clear our boss is in love with her. Thankfully, Lucille's divorce is being fast-tracked through the system."

"As it should be," Tanner agreed. Lucille Lowry, Robyn's mother, had filed for divorce prior to her husband's attempt to kill Robyn to prevent her from testifying against Elan Gifford. The guy was currently in jail after pleading guilty to attempted murder, and awaiting sentencing.

Staring down at his list, he tried to think of what else they'd need.

Sidney finished feeding Lilly and set her down on the floor to roll around and play with her toys.

"Ready to eat?" Colt asked. "Gather around the table."

Slade gave a brief prayer prior to the meal. It warmed Tanner's heart to know Robyn had brought Slade back to his faith.

Tanner dug into the bacon and eggs with gusto. Sidney seemed to enjoy the food, too. He frowned when his phone dinged with an incoming text.

"Crane?" Colt asked, his mouth full of food.

"Yeah. Says he wants a meeting with all of us at nine o'clock." He glanced at his watch. "Thirty minutes."

"That should work," Slade said. "We'll be finished by then."

"Do I get to join the meeting?" Sidney asked.

"Of course." He glanced at her curiously. "We want and need your input regarding the arrangements we're making."

"Does that mean I can check out the next safe house?" She gestured toward the computer. "You didn't show me what you found."

"Sorry about that." He felt bad for excluding her. "You can check it out when we're finished."

"Thanks," Sidney murmured.

"I hereby nominate Tanner for kitchen cleanup duty," Colt announced.

Slade snickered. Tanner groaned. It wasn't like he could argue, since Colt did the majority of the cooking. Mostly because he was obsessed with food. "Yeah, fine. I'll take care of it after the conference call with Crane."

"I can help," Sidney added. "Thanks for cooking breakfast, Colt."

"It's not as if he did that out of the goodness of his heart," Tanner grumbled. "It's only because he's afraid he'll starve to death."

"If I left the cooking to you guys, I just might," Colt retorted.

Tanner finished eating and began clearing the table. At exactly nine o'clock, his phone rang. He placed the phone in the center of the table.

Sidney sat next to him. Beneath the table, her hand clasped his.

He pressed the speaker button, then smiled at Sidney reassuringly. "Boss? We're all here, including the judge," Tanner said. "I have a few items we need before Monday, including the safe house we found about a half mile from the courthouse."

They all heard Crane sigh. "Okay, let me have it."

"Bullet-resistant vests for everyone is at the top of the list," Tanner said. "I want Sidney protected from any further gunfire."

"I can make that work," Crane agreed. "Tell me about this safe house."

Tanner filled him in on the new rental property. "I'll text you the link."

"What else?" Crane asked.

Tanner glanced at the others. "Any way we can refuse to have a deputy in the judge's courtroom during the trial?"

"Doubtful, especially since we have no proof anyone working at the courthouse has been compromised."

"A conveniently broken camera on the third floor with a view of the judge's courtroom on the day she receives a threat isn't enough?" Tanner asked.

Sidney tightened her hand on his, as if silently telling him to cool his temper. He squeezed back and nodded.

"Sometimes technology breaks down, Wilcox. So, no, that's not enough." Crane added, "I have good news to share."

"We could use it," Tanner said.

"What's up, boss?" Colt asked.

"Alonzo Cruz is in federal custody."

Tanner's jaw dropped. "That's excellent news. But can we convince him to testify against Santiago?"

"We've already informed him about Becca Rice agreeing to testify against him and Franco, so he knew he'd be doing hard time. A fact that helped him see the light, so, yeah, he's willing to testify against Santiago."

Tanner grinned as Colt and Slade exchanged a fist bump.

"Even better, he gave us another name," Crane continued. "Does Wade Marcus sound familiar to any of you?"

"Wade Marcus." Tanner glanced at Sidney, who shook her head, as did the others. "No, who is he?"

"That's what we're trying to figure out. According to Cruz, this Marcus character is the guy giving orders about who to target and when. Claims Marcus is working for Santiago."

Tanner sat back in his chair, still holding Sidney's hand. "Thanks for the information—we'll see what we can find out about the guy."

"I'll work on the vests and the safe house," Crane said. "Keep me posted if you find anything."

"Will do." Tanner watched as Colt reached over to end the call. "Sidney?" He glanced at her. "What do you think? Does Wade Marcus work for Quincy Andrews?"

"I don't know," she admitted. "You really think Quincy Andrews is involved?"

It was a fair question—the guy was an officer of the court. Yet the pattern he'd found related to Quincy Andrews's clients was disturbing.

He sounded paranoid even to his own ears. First the deputies, then the defense lawyer.

Paranoid or not, Tanner didn't trust any of them.

FOURTEEN

Overwhelmed with relief in knowing Alonzo Cruz was in custody of the Feds, Sidney focused on the new name that had been identified as a possible link to Santiago.

Wade Marcus. She hadn't recognized the name at first, but now there was something niggling at the back of her mind. Wade Marcus. Had she brought a case against him during her years as a prosecutor? There had been countless criminals she'd prosecuted and sent to jail, too many to remember.

Still, she felt like there was something there, hanging just out of reach.

"Sidney? Are you okay?"

"Huh? Oh, yes, fine." She smiled at

Tanner. They were still holding hands beneath the table and she didn't want to let him go. "Having Cruz in custody and willing to testify against Santiago is huge. I just keep going back to that name, Wade Marcus."

Tanner's gaze sharpened. "I thought you didn't recognize the name?"

"I can't put a face with it, no. But there is something about it that seems familiar." She grimaced. "Unfortunately, I can't tell you why. Maybe someone I ran across during my time as a prosecutor."

"We'll do a search on him, maybe if we find a mug shot that will jar your memory." Tanner released her hand and rose. "In fact, we need to get on that, ASAP."

"Not until you clean the kitchen," Colt objected. "I'll make more coffee."

"Yeah, yeah," Tanner groused. "I didn't forget."

Sidney helped Tanner clean up the

kitchen, then changed Lilly. As much as she wanted to help find Wade Marcus, it was better to let the marshals do that.

The hours dragged by slowly. Normally, Sidney loved having one-on-one time with Lilly. But with the trial looming over her head, it was difficult for her to relax and live in the moment.

The guys never found anything on Wade Marcus, which meant he couldn't have been involved in any of her prosecution cases, or he'd be in the system. Still, there was something about the name that bothered her.

Slade left early on Sunday to pick up the bullet-resistant vests. As much as she hated the thought of wearing it, she was relieved each of the marshals would have the added protection.

With three guys in the safe house, she didn't have any alone time with Tanner. Although he continued to pitch in to help care for Lilly. Each time she watched

Tanner and Lilly together, she lost another small piece of her heart.

Wishing for something she couldn't have.

By the time Monday morning came around, the tension in the safe house was thicker than the snow topping the Rocky Mountains. Each of the three marshals were armed and ready for anything.

It was comforting and unnerving at the same time.

She didn't want to admit how much she dreaded returning to the courtroom to face Santiago. She was hopeful that once Quincy Andrews informed Santiago about the arrest of Alonzo Cruz, the defendant would agree to change his plea.

Yet she didn't get the sense Santiago would accept responsibility. Not unless there was proof linking Wade Marcus to Santiago.

Hence, she needed to be fully prepared to preside over the two-week-long trial. Sidney reminded herself the first day of the trial would be uneventful. The voir dire process would likely take a good portion of the day, maybe even into the following morning. Nothing at all to be nervous about.

Besides, the sooner the trial got underway, the sooner it would be over. And she truly trusted Tanner, and, of course, Colt and Slade, to keep her and Lilly safe.

After feeding and changing the baby, she dressed in the new pantsuit and blazer she'd purchased at Hannah's Boutique. The grim reminder of the gunfire shattering the window only made her more determined to carry out her role as a non-biased judge.

"Don't forget your vest." Tanner brought over the heavy vest and helped her strap it on.

"It's bulky," she noted.

"I know, but necessary. Ready to go?" Tanner looked serious as he reached for both the diaper bag and the car seat.

"Yes." She picked up her briefcase, but Colt took it from her fingers.

"You just worry about Lilly," he drawled. "Slade is going to follow us from Laramie to the Cheyenne federal courthouse. His being behind us should prevent a tail."

"Great." They all crowded in the garage, where Tanner's SUV had been parked since their frenzied escape on Friday. After Tanner had strapped in the car seat, she buckled Lilly in. "Do you want me to sit in the back with her?"

"Yes, Colt is going to drive, so I can keep an eye on things." Tanner hadn't smiled much this morning, and she missed his reassuring attitude.

She placed a hand on his arm. "Tanner, is everything okay? You haven't heard of any new threats or anything, have you?"

"Everything is fine." The corner of his mouth tipped up. "I want to make sure you get to Cheyenne without a problem."

Grateful to know he hadn't been holding out on her, Sidney slid into the back seat next to her daughter. Tanner opened the garage door, then closed it after Colt drove through and joined them in the vehicle.

"Thanks for leaving so early," she said, breaking the silence. "I know the drive normally only takes an hour, so I really appreciate you leaving two and a half hours before court is scheduled to be in session."

"We're going to be taking alternate routes," Tanner cautioned, glancing back at her. "So just know, the drive may take longer than an hour."

"That's fine, as long as I'm there well before court is scheduled to open."

"Don't worry, Sidney," Colt joked. "I'm driving instead of Tanner, just to make sure we don't run late."

"I'm not always late," Tanner protested. "And most of the time it's not my fault if I am."

Their banter eased some of the tension. She played with Lilly, keeping the baby occupied as Colt took the long way to Cheyenne.

"When will we go to the new safe house?" she asked. She also wanted to go and check out the rental property they'd arranged for her to live in, once the trial was over.

"Not until after court adjourns for the day," Tanner said. "Better not to tip our hand ahead of time."

She tugged at the bulky vest. "You really think I need to wear this in court? I doubt anyone will shoot me in the middle of the trial."

"Yes, they are necessary." He turned in his seat to look at her. "I want you to wear it, for me."

How could she refuse? "Okay. I'm glad it won't be obvious beneath my robe."

"Thanks." Tanner turned back to scan the road.

The trip was uneventful. When Sidney saw the sign indicating they were entering the Cheyenne city limits, her stomach tightened.

This was it. They'd be at the courthouse in ten minutes or less.

Crack! The sharp sound of gunfire shattered the silence. The vehicle jerked beneath the impact.

Sidney threw her body over Lilly, hoping to use her own body, with the bullet-resistant vest, to shield her daughter, even as the SUV veered sharply off the road.

"We're hit," Colt said grimly. "Get Slade on the phone ASAP. Tell him the shot came from the southwest."

Sidney gulped, closed her eyes and prayed.

"Slade! We're hit! Shooter is on the southwest side of the road!" Tanner shouted through the speaker.

"I'm coming up behind you now," Slade said calmly.

Tanner realized he was losing his cool and tried to swallow past the hard lump of panic lodged in his throat. The gunfire had taken him by surprise.

Their vehicle being hit was even worse.

Having Sidney and Lilly in danger yet again was wearing on him. He couldn't fail them.

"We're sitting ducks out here…" Slade pulled up beside them, on the side opposite from the source of the gunfire.

"Did you call the local police?" Slade asked through his open window. "The shooter can just as easily try again."

Tanner was frankly surprised there hadn't been more gunfire. He made the 911 call, but refused to stay on the line with the dispatcher. Instead, he called his boss.

"We've been ambushed just off the interstate," Tanner said bluntly. "SUV has been hit in the engine block. Slade is here, but we're out in the open without cover."

Crane muttered something undecipherable under his breath and said, "I'll arrange to have an armored bullet-resistant vehicle driven by another marshal to pick you up. Stay low, give me fifteen minutes."

"Got it." Tanner disconnected from the call, then glanced back at Sidney and Lilly. Sidney was covering most of Lilly's body with hers. "Sidney? We need to get out of the vehicle."

She lifted her head a quarter of an inch, just enough to see him. "Aren't we safer in here?"

"Not if the next bullet hits the gas tank." Tanner didn't like leaving the SUV, but what choice did he have? The vehicle could be used as a weapon against them. "Crawl over Lilly and get out on the side next to Slade's SUV."

"Lilly first," Sidney said, the familiar stubborn glint in her tone. "She's vulnerable back here without me protecting her."

He should have expected this. "Okay, Lilly first." He pushed open his door just enough to ease through. Keeping his head down, he opened the back passenger door.

Sidney released the seat belt holding Lilly's car seat in place. He removed the car seat, baby and all, and set her behind the large rear tire. Sidney quickly joined them, crouching down beside him, her hand protectively resting on Lilly's car seat.

Sandwiched between the two SUVs was the best protection he could offer. And it wasn't nearly enough.

He was glad he'd decided to send Slade to pick up the bullet-resistant vests. It had been a risk, and honestly, he couldn't help but wonder if that maneuver had made it possible for them to be followed.

Or maybe, he was becoming too emotionally involved to think clearly and logically.

If Sidney or Lilly were injured, or worse, as a result of his failure, he'd never forgive himself.

He took a moment to thank God they were all safe and beg for guidance mov-

Laura Scott

ing forward. The prayer helped calm his ragged nerves.

Colt quickly joined them. "Do we stay here? Or get away from the vehicles?" Tanner asked.

"I'm inclined to stay with the vehicles," Colt responded. "I think the gunshot hitting the engine happened by accident, rather than skill."

Tanner wasn't convinced, although he didn't like the idea of heading across the open snowy field, either. Times like this he wished they were hiding in the middle of the mountains, rather than out here in civilization. "Slade?"

"Agree we should stay put."

Tanner reluctantly nodded, hoping the lack of additional gunfire around them indicated the shooter had taken off to avoid being caught.

Still, the thought of someone shooting at the gas tank twisted his gut into knots. He pushed aside the paralyzing thought. "Crane is sending an armored vehicle," he informed them. "When that arrives, we need to convince the driver to stay here, while we take over."

Colt and Slade exchanged a glance. "You don't trust the marshal assigned by our boss?" Colt asked.

"I know I sound paranoid, but I'd feel better if the three of us escort Sidney and Lilly to the courthouse. I don't like the idea of having an unknown person involved." He hesitated, then added, "Even another marshal."

There was a long silence before Slade spoke. "Okay, we'll find a way to make it work."

"Thanks." Tanner knew that in Slade's previous case, local cops had tried to kill his witness, Robyn. Tanner still believed a deputy or two who'd been on duty at the courthouse were also involved with the threats against Sidney.

For all he knew, they were facing a similar situation.

"Do you think the shooter is this Wade

Marcus guy?" Colt asked. "Or has Marcus already replaced Cruz and Franco, finding another idiot to do his dirty work?"

"I don't know." From what Tanner could see, there was no lack of people willing to break the law.

He shifted a bit as his thigh muscles were cramping up. The other guys must be suffering the same malady. Only Sidney was sitting on the ground, hovering over Lilly while playing with her, in an attempt to keep her safely covered by her protective gear.

The armored vehicle arrived fifteen minutes later. Tanner could tell Sidney was concerned about the delay in getting to the courthouse, but to her credit, she didn't say anything. Good thing they'd given themselves extra time to get to Cheyenne.

The marshal pulled up behind Slade's SUV. Tanner carried Lilly's car seat, keeping Sidney in front of him as they approached. Sidney took over from there, ensuring Lilly's car seat was securely fastened before she climbed in beside her.

"Marshal Valencia? Do you have a minute to talk, privately?" Slade asked.

The marshal looked confused, but did as Slade requested. Tanner noticed the guy left the keys in the ignition.

"He's not going to like this," Colt muttered, taking Valencia's place behind the wheel. "And we'll likely hear from Crane about it, too."

Tanner didn't care if Valencia or Crane liked it. Keeping Sidney and Lilly safe was their only priority.

Anyone trying to get to them would have to go through him first.

"We're good to go," Slade said, sliding into the back seat on the other side of Lilly's car seat. "He's mad, but he'll stay behind."

"Let's get out of here," Tanner said urgently.

"Straight to the courthouse," Sidney added.

"Yes, ma'am." Colt hit the gas and the armored vehicle lurched forward.

Minutes later, Colt pulled up directly in front of the courthouse. The moment Tanner pushed open his door a shrieking siren went off from within the building.

"What is that?" Colt asked.

"The courthouse alarm." Sidney craned her neck trying to see past Slade. "I've only heard it once before, when an inmate attempted to escape."

The knot in Tanner's gut tightened. "Do you think this alarm is also due to an escape attempt? What if Santiago is involved?"

Sidney paled. "Maybe. Although I don't understand why he would do something like this since it could result in a mistrial, which means the entire process would start all over again, possibly with another judge and another jury. Although the federal prosecutor would be the same. Why

294 Rocky Mountain Standoff

would he take the risk of having an extended sentence?"

"I don't know," Tanner admitted.

"It could be some other criminal," Slade pointed out. "Not Santiago."

"Yeah." But Tanner didn't think so. "I wonder if the threats were more about setting the stage for an escape attempt, rather than influencing the outcome of a trial." Regardless of the reason, he didn't like it. "Stay here. I'll check it out."

"No, wait!" Sidney sounded upset. "I need to get inside with Lilly."

"Not if Santiago is the one who escaped. Let me find out what's happening." Tanner slammed the door shut as a way to prevent more arguing.

Time was of the essence. He took the courthouse steps two at a time, reaching the top in seconds. He was met by a deputy. Thankfully, not one of the guys he'd gotten into trouble.

"What's going on?" Tanner demanded.

"I have Judge Logan here. She's scheduled to be in court in twenty minutes."

"Not happening," the deputy informed him. "A prisoner escaped, and the place is on lockdown."

"Who?"

"Manuel Santiago," the deputy confirmed. "We found a deputy handcuffed and dressed in an orange jumpsuit in one of the holding cells."

Just as he'd suspected. Tanner spun around, intending to return to the armored truck, when he caught a glimpse of another deputy walking quickly away from the courthouse, his hat pulled down low over his brow, his face hidden behind his hand as he spoke softly into the radio on his collar.

No, it couldn't be. Could it? Tanner didn't hesitate—he took off running after the cop, believing with every fiber of his being the guy was really Santiago.

And that he'd somehow gotten out of the courthouse before the lockdown.

FIFTEEN

"Where is he going?" Sidney watched in shock as Tanner took off running. She reached up to grab Slade's shoulder. "One of you need to back him up!"

The two marshals glanced at each other, obviously not sure about what was going on.

"This car is bullet-resistant, right?" They nodded. "Okay, then, we're fine here with just one of you. I'm worried about Tanner—he needs backup!"

"I'll go." Slade shoved the open door and leaped from the car. He slammed the door shut then sprinted after Tanner.

Colt sat for a minute, then put the vehicle into Drive and headed down the street in the same direction the two marshals had taken. Their progress was slow, as there was traffic to contend with.

"Hurry," she urged. "I don't have a good feeling about this."

"I'm trying," Colt said in a grim tone. "I agree—something's not right."

No sooner had the words left his mouth than they heard the sharp report of gunfire.

No! Tanner! Sidney craned her neck, trying to see where he was. She caught a glimpse of him jumping forward and taking a deputy down to the ground.

A deputy? Or the escaped prisoner?

Slade caught up to them and helped slap cuffs on the deputy's wrists. Colt found a spot to pull over, so they could see what was happening.

When Tanner and Slade hauled the man upright, Sidney gasped. "Santiago!"

"Well, now, isn't that interesting?" Colt drawled as a goofy grin crossed his face. "Trust Tanner to catch the bad guy."

Sidney was proud of Tanner for his accomplishment, but was still worried about the gunshot. She searched desperately for blood, but didn't see anything.

Had his bullet-resistant vest worked? She hoped and prayed that was the case.

Then she noticed Tanner bent over, pressing a hand to his left side. "Colt? He's hurt!"

Colt was already on the phone with the 911 dispatcher, requesting an ambulance and backup to their location, roughly ten blocks from the courthouse.

Sidney shifted in her seat, wanting to go to Tanner, yet hesitant to leave Lilly alone with Colt. The vehicle was armored but she couldn't bear to leave her daughter.

Even if Santiago was captured, the shooter from a half hour ago was still out there somewhere.

As she watched, Slade took a firm hold on Santiago and said something to Tanner. Tanner nodded and grimaced, then walked toward the vehicle.

"You were hit?" Colt asked, taking the words right out of her mouth.

"Yeah." Tanner gingerly slid into the passenger seat. He glanced back at her. "Wearing body armor was a good idea, though. The vest absorbed most of the impact."

"Most of the impact?" She didn't know much about how the vest worked.

"Still hurts when you're hit, especially at close range," Colt said with a frown. "An ambulance should be here any minute."

"I'm fine," Tanner insisted, although based on the pained expression his face, she didn't believe him. "Slade is taking Santiago back to the courthouse. I told him we'd meet him there."

Before Colt could drive away, a squad car pulled up, a female officer behind the wheel, and blocked him in. Colt groaned and shut down the vehicle. "I don't think we're going anywhere soon."

"But I have to get to court," Sidney protested. "Especially now that we know Santiago escaped! I have to deal with the jury members and talk to both the prosecutor and Santiago's defense attorney."

"We'll get there," Tanner promised. "Colt? Can't you sweet-talk your way out of here?"

"Me?" Colt glared at him, then pushed open the driver's-side door to approach the squad. The female officer came out join him.

It didn't take long for the female officer to open the back of her squad car, so Slade could shove Santiago inside. Then he climbed in next to the female deputy. Raising a hand to Colt, the deputy pulled away from the curb.

"We're all going back to the courthouse," Colt informed them. "At least the marshals are getting credit for capturing Santiago."

She shivered, glad that Santiago was in the squad car and not in their armored vehicle. The ride to the courthouse took longer than it should have, thanks to the dozens of police and sheriff's deputies who'd descended upon the place. The crowd should have made her feel safer, but it didn't.

When Colt was able to park close enough to the structure, she went to work unbuckling the seat belt holding Lilly's car seat in place. When Tanner slid out and opened the back to help her, she frowned.

"You really need to let the EMTs take a look at you, Tanner." He looked pale with tiny brackets of pain lining his mouth. "What if you have internal bleeding?"

"Time for that later." He reached for the car seat and gently pulled Lilly out.

"And you called me stubborn?" She slid across the seat to join him.

"I'm fine, let's concentrate on getting you inside." He pushed past the crowd to take the steps up to the door.

Glancing back over her shoulder, she noted Colt was right behind her. Beyond him, she saw the female officer and Slade, one on each side of Santiago as they led him, up the stairs as well.

When they reached the door, the sheriff's deputies gave Tanner a hard time.

"No one in or out," the burly one said.

"I'm the one who captured Santiago," Tanner responded. "Judge Logan needs to get inside. Now!"

The deputies looked surprised at his comment, and then appeared upset when they saw Santiago dressed in a deputy's uniform.

"I don't believe it," the burly guy muttered.

"Yeah, how did he get past you, anyway?" Tanner asked. "Good thing I saw him on the street and took off after him."

"And got shot while bringing him down," Sidney added, frustrated with their attitude. She was determined to launch a full-blown investigation into how Santiago managed to escape. Not to mention, the other lapses in security that she'd experienced over the last week. "Please let us through."

The deputies reluctantly stepped aside. Tanner, Sidney, Lilly and Colt went through the security process of being screened and scanned before they were allowed inside the courthouse lobby.

It seemed like years rather than days since she'd last been inside. Then again, it could be that she was seeing everything with new eyes.

"I need to know what happened with Santiago," she said when they were on the elevator heading up to the third floor. She looked between Tanner and Colt. "Can you help with that?"

"I'll find out," Colt said. "Tanner needs to stay with you."

"Tanner also needs medical care." She scowled at him. "I saw you stumble back when you were shot, Tanner. Please allow the EMTs to examine you. As a favor to me."

Those moments when Tanner had been

shot had made her realize how much she cared about him. What if he hadn't been wearing the vest? The idea of him lying bleeding on the sidewalk made her shiver.

He sighed when she tossed his words back in his face. "Soon," he promised. "Let's find out what happened here first."

She led the way down the hall toward her chambers. The only evidence of the explosion was the new section of flooring that stood out against the older tiles and the door, which had been repaired. Thankfully, her key still worked.

They'd barely gotten Lilly settled when there was a knock on the door leading in from the courtroom. Tanner held up a hand, then went over to answer it.

"I need to see Judge Logan right away." Recognizing Darnell Chance's voice, she gently nudged Tanner aside to speak to the prosecutor.

"I'm here, Mr. Chance. What's the problem?"

"I'm formally requesting you refrain

from declaring a mistrial," Darnell announced. "Santiago needs to pay for his crimes now more than ever."

"You shouldn't be in here, making statements off the record," she chided.

Darnell scowled. "I'm happy to make my case on the record, Your Honor."

"I'll call the court to order in thirty minutes. Have the clerk notify defense counsel." She gestured for the prosecutor to leave. When he went back into the courtroom, she shut the door and sighed. "I really have to convene, if only to formally adjourn the proceedings for the day."

Before Tanner could say anything in response, there was another knock at the door. Tanner opened the main door, and stepped back to allow Colt in. "What did you find out about how Santiago escaped?"

"They found Deputy Archie Burrows tied up in his own handcuffs and wearing prison orange." Colt spread his hands.

"So far, he's claiming Santiago overpowered him, but no one believes that."

"What do the cameras say?" Sidney asked. "They must have the incident on video."

"That's just it," Colt said. "The camera inside the holding cell wasn't working."

Another camera out of commission? She glanced at Tanner, who shook his head.

"Yeah, that's not a coincidence. I'm sure Santiago threatened him or his family, maybe his sixteen-year-old daughter. Although, again, he should have come to us if that was the case." The way Tanner kept a hand pressed to his lower left side concerned her.

"They have taken Burrows into custody as an accomplice, until this can get sorted out," Colt added. "Which is probably for the best."

She hated knowing that the deputy who'd replaced Paul Kramer had helped Santiago escape.

And Santiago would have gotten away with it, if not for Tanner's quick work.

Just one more thing to admire about Tanner.

And Sidney realized once again how much she'd miss him, now that the danger was over.

Tanner did his best to ignore the throbbing pain in his side. "I agree Burrows should be locked up, but I hope they keep him far away from Santiago." It wouldn't surprise Tanner if Santiago managed to make good on his threats against the deputy's family.

If that was why he'd helped the guy escape in the first place.

"Colt, will you arrange for the EMTs to be brought up here to examine Tanner?"

Sidney's request made him frown. "I can do that later. Santiago might be back in custody but the shooter who hit our SUV is still out there."

"Yes, but there's no way he's getting in here," Sidney protested.

"We don't know that for sure," Tanner argued. "What if Wade Marcus is an attorney? Or an investigator? Or another cop?"

Sidney's gaze darted fearfully toward Lilly, but then she squared her shoulders. "I'm sure we will be safe enough here in my chambers."

Another knock at the hallway door drew his attention. Tanner wasn't surprised to see Slade standing there, with a couple of EMTs.

"They need to examine you before they can return to their station," Slade informed him. "So how about you just cooperate, the way you'd expect us to?"

His buddy had a point. Since they were here, he waved them in. "Fine. But I'm not going to the hospital."

The EMTs rolled their eyes.

"I need to change Lilly," Sidney said,

taking the baby into the restroom, no doubt to give him privacy.

He shed the vest and gingerly lifted his shirt high enough for the EMTs to see the dark bruise already forming over his entire left side.

Colt was right—getting shot at close range even while wearing a vest, hurt like the dickens.

He gritted his teeth as they probed the bruise. "This is roughly where your spleen is," the older and hopefully more experienced EMT informed him. "You may have ruptured it, or at the very least, bruised it."

It hurt enough to be ruptured, but he wasn't leaving. "I feel fine."

They proceeded to take a set of vital signs.

"Your blood pressure and pulse are both stable." The EMT shrugged. "However, it could take a while for a young healthy person to have symptoms of blood loss.

You really should come to the ER for a CT scan."

"If the pain gets worse or I feel light-headed, I will." Tanner rebuttoned his shirt.

Sidney came out of the bathroom with Lilly, her green gaze full of concern. "I really wish you'd go now, Tanner, rather than when it's an emergency."

He waited until the EMTs had packed up their gear and left her chambers. "How much longer will you be here?"

She grimaced. "I don't know. I haven't heard if Quincy Andrews is available for a hearing. I also need to let any jury members who managed to get here before the lockdown leave. For sure, the trial isn't moving forward today. Not now."

He nodded. "I'll stick around until you're ready to go. I assume there isn't anything else on your calendar?"

"No. Just the trial." She pulled her robes on over her clothes and the vest. He was grateful she was still wearing it.

He didn't put anything past anyone at this point.

"Okay, slight change of plans." Tanner glanced between Slade and Colt. "I'd like one of you to stay here with Lilly. I'm not at one hundred percent, so it might be better if I'm in the courtroom with one of you helping to cover me."

"I'll do it," Colt offered. He grinned. "Babies love me."

Sidney opened her mouth as if to protest, but then nodded. "Thank you, Colt. Okay, I need to get some work done."

Tanner and Slade followed her into the courtroom. There was a deputy on duty, and Slade immediately crossed over to talk to the guy.

"Your Honor? May I be heard?" The prosecuting attorney asked.

Sidney frowned. "Not until we are on the record." She glanced at Bruce Matthews, the clerk replacing Becca. "Where is defense counsel? Is he planning to be here?"

"My understanding is that defense counsel is still waiting to talk to his client," Matthews said. "He promised to be here within the hour."

Sidney glanced at the clock on the wall. "Okay, then we will reconvene in another thirty minutes. Bruce? Can you please release any and all jurors who have reported for duty today?"

"Of course. Should I have them return tomorrow?"

She hesitated, then shook her head. "No, I don't think we'll be ready to go that quickly. Let them know we'll be in touch and thank them for their service."

"But, Your Honor," Chance blurted, "I'm ready to go to trial!"

"Your position on this is duly noted." Tanner could tell Sidney was irritated with him. "But there's nothing more we can do until defense counsel is ready."

"Defense counsel should be here," Darnell Chance argued.

Tanner wondered what the prosecutor

was so concerned about. What did he care if the trial moved forward today, a week from today or a month from today?

As long as Santiago was locked up—and after this latest stunt, he would probably be placed in solitary confinement—it didn't matter when the trial took place.

Keeping Santiago in jail, where he belonged, was the most important thing.

"I'll be back in thirty minutes," Sidney said, rising to her feet. Tanner noticed there was far less formality when they weren't on record with jury members or defendants in attendance. "Bruce, please track down Quincy Andrews."

"Will do," the clerk promised.

Tanner moved toward Sidney as she stepped down from the bench. He didn't take a deep breath of relief until she was back inside her chambers.

"That didn't take long," Colt said.

"It's only a brief recess," Tanner explained. "The clerk is trying to find Quincy Andrews."

"Maybe after he heard about Santiago's escape, he skipped town," Colt mused. He continued playing with Lilly, entertaining her with her rattle. "I can't say that I'd blame him."

"No, he's a career defense attorney." Tanner didn't for one minute believe the guy had skipped town. "I think he's made a good living off guys like Santiago, Franco and whoever else he's defended over the years. Why on earth would he stop now?"

"I agree with Tanner. Andrews would get in trouble if he left a client hanging right before trial," Sidney pointed out. "Hopefully, he's doing his best to convince Santiago to make a deal."

Tanner was definitely in favor of that outcome. When his phone rang, he recognized Crane's number and groaned. He put the call on speaker.

"Yeah, boss?"

"Just wanted you to know the locals just arrested Wade Marcus."

"They did?" Tanner glanced at Sidney. "Is he willing to testify against Santiago?"

"Yep. He agreed to turn on his boss, especially when he learned we had Cruz in custody. And you should know, Marcus is a private investigator."

"PI for who?" he demanded. "Andrews?"

"Yes, at least in the past. No indication Marcus had been used by Andrews recently. And I still don't think Andrews told the guy to go out and kill people."

"That's why I recognized his name," Sidney said. "I think he testified in a trial a while back, maybe nine months ago?"

Tanner knew the slick attorney wasn't as clean as a whistle. "I'm glad to hear this, boss. This means the judge and her daughter are no longer in danger."

"Yep. I also hear you've been injured and are refusing treatment. I want you seen at the local hospital before the end of the day, understand?"

"Yes, sir." He disconnected from the

line and locked gazes with Sidney. He was overwhelmed with relief to know she and Lilly were no longer in danger.

Yet he also didn't want to leave them.

SIXTEEN

"I'm so glad they found and arrested
Wade Marcus." The news was stagger-
ing. Difficult to imagine a private investigator turning criminal.

It seemed her nightmare was over. That
she and Lilly were finally safe. The little
girl gazed up at her from the car seat, her
dark eyes curious.

Sidney's heart melted. All she'd wanted
was to provide Lilly a good home. But
over the last few days, the innocent baby
had been in danger.

Not to mention, Sidney didn't have a
home any longer. She hadn't even begun
the process of getting her homeowner's
insurance to pay for the damage. Lilly's
bedroom, most of her clothes and toys

were gone. Granted, Tanner had arranged for a rental house, but it wouldn't be ready to be lived in for several days. At least not until she'd bought a crib and changing table for the nursery.

Was it fair for her to continue with the adoption process? Or should she call Tabitha, Lilly's social worker, and see if there was another foster family who would take her in? Now that Lilly's medical needs have been stabilized, she felt certain there would be plenty of options.

"Sidney? Marcus being arrested and willing to testify is good news." Tanner searched her gaze questioningly. He was so in tune to her on every level, he must have realized she was having doubts. "There's nothing for you to worry about. Everything is going to work out just fine."

"I know." Oddly, now that the danger was over, the other mundane tasks of picking up the pieces of her life seemed overwhelming. "Thanks to you I have a place to live, but I still need to buy replacement items for Lilly. And for me. And arrange for child care…" She couldn't finish as the image of Camella's dead body flashed in her mind.

So much death and destruction. And for what? Money?

No, freedom. She felt certain this had been Santiago's plan all along. Threaten people and follow through on those threats enough to enable a daring escape from the courthouse.

"You can use the safe house we've arranged until the rental property is all set." Tanner's comment interrupted her thoughts. "We originally had the rental agreement starting after the trial, but we'll try to move that up."

"Are you sure?" It was one less thing for her to worry about.

"Absolutely. Focus on finishing up what you need to do here, okay? We'll escort you safely out of the courthouse."

"It's a good plan," Slade agreed. "In the meantime, I need to head downstairs to give my statement about how we captured Santiago." Slade frowned at Tanner. "You'll need to do that, too."

"I know. And I will." Tanner once again put a hand over the bruise on his side.

"Will you promise to go to the hospital as soon as I wrap things up here?" She pinned Tanner with a narrow gaze. "You look like you might topple over at any moment."

"I'm not going to fall down, it just hurts," Tanner said defensively.

She simply lifted an eyebrow and waited.

"Yes, I will go as soon as you finish up here," he finally agreed.

"Good." She glanced at the phone, wondering when Bruce would let her know the attorneys were ready and present in the courtroom.

Sidney had always loved the law. The checks and balances. The scales of justice. Not that the law was black and white, because it wasn't. But she'd always enjoyed her work.

Today, she couldn't wait to get out of the courthouse. It occurred to her that she probably needed to take a short leave of absence. Her calendar was basically clear for the next two weeks of trial.

She needed time to regroup. To put her personal life in order.

Her gaze fell once again on Lilly. Despite the tiny voice telling her it might be better for the baby, she couldn't bear the idea of handing over Lilly to someone else.

She wanted to go through with the adoption.

Her phone buzzed and she picked up the receiver. "Yes?"

"Defense counsel and the prosecutor are both present, Your Honor," Bruce said.

"Thanks. I'll be right in." She replaced the phone and stood. "This shouldn't take long."

"I'll stay with Lilly," Colt offered.

"I'm coming with you," Tanner added.

She wanted to argue that at this point, it was overkill, but she let it go. At least Santiago wouldn't be in the courtroom this time. He was on strict lockdown after his escape.

The two attorneys stood as she entered the room. She took the three steps up to the bench and sat. "We are here to discuss the matter of the US federal government versus Manuel Santiago." As she spoke, the court reporter recorded the proceedings. "Mr. Andrews, are you aware of your client's recent escape from this courthouse?"

"I am now, yes." Quincy Andrews stood. "I had difficulty getting in and through security, so I am just now learning of these events."

She glared at him. "Have you spoken to your client?"

"No, Your Honor. I wasn't permitted to speak with him personally and privately in the pretrial holding area."

Prosecutor Chance shot to his feet. "Your Honor, defense counsel has kept us waiting for over an hour. Given his client's status as a flight risk, I'm sure he could have had a brief conversation with him about whether he intends to continue with trial."

"I agree." Sidney batted down a wave of frustration.

The prosecutor added, "Judge, the government is ready to move forward with presenting the evidence we have gathered against Mr. Santiago." Chance looked pointedly at Andrews. "Including evidence pertaining to the new charges we plan to file this afternoon related to Mr. Santiago's escape and the threats he's leveraged against government employees."

She lifted a hand, indicating she didn't need to hear any more. "I'm aware of your stance on this issue, Mr. Chance." She pierced Andrews with another stare. "And I agree with the prosecutor. You've had plenty of time to discuss this case with your client. After the stunt he'd pulled, there was no reason to risk putting him in a room with you, unsupervised by law enforcement."

"Your Honor," Andrews protested. "Law enforcement was with him when he escaped and clearly—"

"Enough." She cut him off. At first she'd thought a mistrial was the way to go. But after this, she changed her mind.

After a long moment, she spoke. "I am inclined to declare a continuance of this trial, with a brief recess over the next two days. In that forty-eight-hour time frame, I expect the prosecutor will have several additional charges filed against Mr. Santiago." She waited a beat, then said, "Mr. Andrews, I sincerely hope you can convince your client to change his plea and to forfeit his request for a trial."

"I can't do that without talking to my client privately," Andrews responded.

She ignored him. "I also expect the two of you to work out a deal. Mr. Andrews, I hardly believe a trial will result in Mr. Santiago obtaining the freedom he so clearly desires. Mr. Chance, you have leverage you can use especially considering these recent events to bring this issue to a swift close."

The two men didn't say anything in response.

Satisfied that she'd given them both a job to do, she pounded her gavel. "Court is adjourned for the rest of the day."

As she rose to her feet, the two attorneys glanced at each other in a way that gave her hope they'd reach a plea bargain. Likely Santiago agreeing to a life sentence as long as the prosecutor took the death penalty off the table.

The same arrangement she'd tried to get them to agree to months ago.

On the way back to her chambers, Tanner whispered, "Way to rule the courtroom, Judge."

A blush heated her cheeks. "Thanks, but this is what I do every day, you just aren't here to see it." She sobered, realizing that she wasn't going to have Tanner around for protection much longer.

Considering how anxious she was to get rid of him back in early December, she hated the idea of him leaving.

But, of course, he had a job to do, just like she did. They were always going to be two ships passing in the night. Each moving to different destinations.

"Slade called," Colt said as they entered the room. "Tanner, you're up next. They want you down to give your statement."

He frowned. "In a few minutes."

She shrugged out of her robes and hung them on the hanger in the narrow closet behind her. "You may as well go now, Tanner. I may have to feed Lilly again, anyway."

The door between the courtroom and her chambers abruptly opened. She turned with a frown. The clerks knew better than to simply barge into a judge's chambers.

Then she froze when she saw Bruce Matthews standing there, holding a gun. "Throw down your weapons," he demanded. "Or I'll shoot the judge right here, right now."

"Bruce?" She gaped at him in shock. "What's wrong? Why are you doing this?"

"Now!" The clerk's gaze never wavered from Colt and Tanner, both of whom had remained still.

"Easy," Tanner cautioned. "You're not going to get away with this. Every law-enforcement official in the building is on high alert after the escape this morning."

"Drop the guns!" Bruce shouted.

"Okay, okay." Colt gingerly pulled his weapon out of his holster. "Don't get trigger-happy. I'm dropping my gun to the floor."

Sidney noticed Tanner's mouth tightening, but he, too, reached for his weapon. Fearing for Lilly's safety, she subtly picked up the infant carrier, and set it on the floor behind her desk.

If Bruce started shooting, she wanted Lilly to be safe. If only she'd taken off her protective vest, to drape it over the baby.

"Bruce, please," she begged as Tanner also dropped his weapon. "You heard what happened in the courtroom. Santiago will likely cut a deal. There's no reason for you to do this. The danger is over."

"The judge is right, Matthews," Tanner said. "If Santiago or his men threatened you or your family, then we can add those charges to the new ones the prosecutor will be bringing against him."

"It's too late." Bruce looked a bit wild. "Don't you understand? It's too late!"

"Whoa, what's too late?" Tanner took another step forward. "You haven't broken any laws yet. There's time to step back from this."

Sidney could tell Bruce wasn't hearing Tanner. He glanced around wildly, his gaze finally resting on her. "You!"

Venom dripped from his tone. "This is all your fault!"

In that moment, Sidney truly believed Matthews wasn't in his right mind. She held out a hand, willing him to understand. "Talk to me, Bruce. What is my fault? Did Santiago threaten your family? Your daughter? Is that it? You should know the US Marshals will offer you protection if that's the case." She didn't dare glance at Tanner, who was inching his way closer to Matthews. Deep down, she knew Tanner would risk his life for her and Lilly, and jump in front of the clerk's gun, if necessary.

And in that moment she realized she didn't just care about Tanner.

She'd fallen in love with him. And didn't want to lose him.

Please, keep us safe, Lord. Please!

"Bruce, we really need you to put down your gun, so we can talk this through. Of course, we want your family to be safe and the US Marshals can certainly place them in protective custody."

"It's too late!" Bruce screamed so loudly this time, Lilly began to wail. "They already murdered her! Josie is dead! And it's all because of you!"

"No, it's not!" Sidney shouted back, a move that startled him. As the muzzle of the gun moved toward her, Tanner rushed forward and grabbed the weapon, yanking it upright in the nick of time. A gunshot rang out and the bullet slammed into the ceiling.

"No-o-o-o," Bruce wailed, as Colt joined Tanner in wrestling the clerk to the ground. Tanner spun toward her.

"Are you okay? You're not hit?"

She shook her head. "I'm okay, he didn't get me." Then she glanced down at Lilly, who was still crying. "We're both fine."

Tanner had to borrow Colt's handcuffs to restrain Bruce. The man was sobbing now, his entire body shaking.

She glanced at Tanner with a frown.

"Bruce, what's wrong? Tell us where your wife and daughter are, and we'll make sure they're safe."

"Dead," Bruce said between sobs. "My daughter is dead."

They'd killed a sixteen-year-old girl? Sidney closed her eyes and bent her head. No wonder Bruce had acted irrationally. He'd been awash in grief.

It was yet another murder that could be attributed to Santiago, but knowing that the man would spend the rest of his time behind bars for his crimes didn't change the outcome.

Too many innocent people had died. Bruce blamed her, and maybe he was right.

What if she'd just recused herself from Santiago's trial and assigned it to someone else? Would Camella and Bruce's daughter both still be alive?

Tears pricked her eyes. Yes, they would. Although the problem of Santiago would have fallen on someone else.

"Don't do this, Sidney." Tanner put his arm around her and gently pulled her close. "Don't go down the what-if path. I've been there and done that, and it doesn't change anything."

"So much death and destruction," she whispered. "I can hardly stand it."

"I know, but despite Matthews's wild accusations, this is Santiago's fault, not yours."

"If I'd have handed off the trial to someone else…"

"People still would have died," he said firmly. "Because Santiago was determined to evade justice."

Tanner was right. Logically, she knew he was right. But emotionally, the devastation would haunt her for a long time.

Lilly's crying increased in volume. She pulled herself together and turned to attend to the baby. Colt dragged Matthews from the room, pushing him into the arms of the deputies who'd responded to the gunshot hitting the ceiling of her chambers.

"Shh, it's okay. We're fine." She lifted Lilly out of the carrier and cuddled her close. "There's nothing to be afraid of."

Tanner stood, then swayed, beads of sweat popping out on his forehead.

A ripple of panic washed over her. She shifted the baby to her left arm, and shoved Tanner toward her desk chair. "Sit down before you faint."

"I'm fine," he said, only this time, his tone was unconvincing.

"You don't look fine. Colt? You might want to call that ambulance back."

"No ambulance." Tanner's voice was stronger now. "Let's just get out of here. You can drop me off at the hospital after we take Sidney and Lilly to the safe house."

"How about we drop you off at the hospital first?" She was growing annoyed with his stubbornness. "You look as if a strong wind would blow you flat on your face."

"She's right, Tanner. You're probably bleeding internally." Colt looked at him in concern. "Let's go. I can probably get you to the hospital faster if I drive you myself."

Sidney was already dressing Lilly in her pink snowsuit. For the first time ever, Tanner didn't offer to take the infant carrier or the diaper bag.

The ripple of panic grew into a massive tidal wave. Tanner must be worse off than he wanted to admit.

"Did you break something open when you tackled Bruce?" She yanked on her coat, shouldered the diaper bag and lifted Lilly and the car seat with both hands. "Because you look really bad, Tanner."

"Maybe." He staggered to his feet, and lurched toward the door. "Let's go."

Sidney exchanged a worried look with Colt. The marshal grabbed Tanner's arm to hold him steady. "If you fall, I'm calling 911," Colt threatened.

"I won't fall." Tanner's voice was firm, but the sheen of sweat covering his forehead told a different story.

She followed the two men into the hallway, pushing past the deputies. Several called out to her, to stop and provide statements about what happened in her chambers, but she shook her head. "Later," she said. "This marshal needs to get emergency medical care ASAP."

The deputies looked frustrated, but no one stopped them as they got onto the elevator. Tanner leaned against the wall, clearly needing the extra support.

"Do you know where the hospital is?" she asked Colt, keeping an eye on Tanner.

"Yeah. Don't worry, I won't get lost."

She nodded and followed Colt and Tanner outside. Her steps slowed when she realized the SUV wasn't here, leaving the armored truck as their only method of transportation. "Do you have the keys?"

Colt nodded and opened the passenger door. Tanner struggled to get in, needing a boost from Colt.

She quickly buckled Lilly's car seat in place, then sat behind Tanner. Leaning forward, she found him sitting with his eyes closed.

"Hurry," she urged Colt. He nodded grimly, and hit the gas. One good thing about Cheyenne—there wasn't a lot of midday traffic to hold them up.

The hospital emergency sign loomed ahead. "We're almost there, Tanner. Stay with us."

"I'm okay." His voice was so soft she could barely hear him.

He wasn't okay. Colt pulled up in front of the ER, then threw the gearshift into Park and ran inside the building, returning seconds later with two hospital personnel and a gurney.

"He's losing consciousness," Colt said urgently. "He might be bleeding internally from being shot at close range while wearing a bullet-resistant vest."

"Let's get him inside."

Tanner didn't protest when the three men lifted him out of the car and set him on the gurney. Her heart lodged painfully in her throat, she watched helplessly as Tanner was whisked away.

SEVENTEEN

Tanner heard voices but couldn't understand the words. His entire body hurt, and the scent of antiseptic was sharp. He tried to move, but his arms and legs weren't working very well. What happened? The last thing he remembered was being in a car.

He didn't like this feeling of not being in control.

"Mr. Wilcox? Squeeze my hand if you can hear me."

Now he could understand, and he tried to do as the woman asked. He managed to squeeze her fingers. He pried open his eyelids, but the bright lights pained him.

"You're in the hospital," the female

voice continued. "You've had surgery, and are in the recovery area."

Surgery? Alarm surged through him, and he forced his eyes open, despite the glare. A pleasant face swam above him, a woman dressed in scrubs.

"What surgery?" His throat was sore, his mouth dry. He couldn't remember feeling this awful in his life.

"Would you like some ice chips?"

"Yes. Please." He forced the words through his sandpaper-lined throat. She gave him a few ice chips from a cup, and despite feeling ridiculous at being fed by another adult, the ice instantly cooled his throat. "What surgery?"

The pleasant face turned serious. "I believe the trauma surgeon removed a hematoma from your abdomen. I'll have him come and talk to you, okay?"

"Hematoma?" Why didn't these people speak English?

"Blood clot," she clarified. "The good

news is that they didn't have to remove your spleen."

He'd have to take her word on that, since he wasn't sure what the purpose of a spleen was. Logically, it would make sense that God had given humans a spleen for a reason, and that removing it might cause a problem.

At least he knew where he was and what had happened to him. It was disconcerting to wake up in the hospital, even more so to realize a surgeon had cut him open.

Now that he was thinking about it, the pain seemed more centered on his left side. The side where he'd been hit by Santiago's bullet. And the same side where he'd felt a little pop when he'd tackled Matthews.

He must have broken something open. Ignoring the pain, he wondered where Sidney and Lilly were. He had to believe Colt had taken them to the safe house that had been arranged. Colt was a good marshal, and he'd keep an eye on them.

He must have faded out, because the next thing he knew, he was being pushed down the hall. "Here's your new room," the pleasant-faced nurse said. "The surgeon should be in within the next hour or so, to update you."

"Didn't you say that before?" Tanner hoped he wasn't losing it.

"Yes, but he was called in to another emergency," she explained. "Here's your call light, so you can let the nursing staff know if you need anything."

"How long do I have to stay here?"

"That's up to the surgeon. Take care now." In a flash, Pleasant Face was gone.

"Tanner, how are you feeling?"

Huh? He turned his head to see Sidney standing beside his bed. Now he felt certain he was losing it. "When did you get here?"

"I've been waiting for about an hour, as soon as we heard you were out of surgery." She cupped both her hands around his. "I was so worried about you. I'm really glad to see you're doing so well."

Doing well was a relative term, but he was more interested in the fact that she'd come here to see him. "And Lilly?"

"She's here, sleeping at the moment in her car seat." Her smile was gentle. "Colt should be here soon. I'm sure you can guess where he is."

"Getting something to eat." He glanced instinctively at the clock on the wall across from him. The time was three thirty in the afternoon, based on the sunshine outside.

"Exactly." Sidney laughed, then her expression turned serious. "They were very concerned about the damage to your spleen. The surgeon said that if you had waited any longer, he might have been forced to remove it."

"You spoke to the surgeon?" He was surprised they'd discussed his case with her. Not that he minded—in fact, he was touched that she'd come here to be with him.

"Well, Colt did, but he had the call on speaker so I could listen."

That made sense. "You know more than I do."

"Tanner, you lost so much blood, they gave you a transfusion of two units of packed red-blood cells. You should have come in to be seen sooner."

"Better late than never." Personally, he was glad he'd waited, considering Bruce Matthews had threatened to kill her. Remembering the scene in her chambers made him frown. "How did Bruce get a gun into the courthouse, anyway?"

She frowned. "Apparently he went in over the weekend, claiming I needed paperwork. The deputy let him in without going through the metal detector."

The news was appalling. "That's the third mistake they made, each one nearly costing your life." He winced as he unintentionally turned his body toward her. "I want the deputy disciplined for that."

"Easy, Tanner." She tightened her grip on his hand. "I've already requested a full investigation into the security breach. This latest incident will be added to the mix." She hesitated, then continued, "Unfortunately, several of these deputies will lose their jobs over this."

They should, as their lax security was unacceptable. But he didn't voice his opinion. It was never easy to know people would lose their jobs, their livelihood, yet he couldn't defend what they'd done. Or rather, not done. One security lapse was bad enough. But more than one, over a short period of time, was outrageous.

"Tanner, don't think about that now. Your only job is to recuperate from this surgery."

He couldn't seem to stop thinking about it. "What about the trial?"

A shadow crossed her features. "I haven't heard from defense counsel yet, but I know the prosecutor has already filed the additional charges against Santiago. Archie Burrows finally admitted that he helped Santiago escape because he received a photo of one of Santiago's men standing next to his wife."

"Which of Santiago's men?"

"Alonzo Cruz. Must have been taken prior to Cruz's arrest." Lilly began to whine, so she released his hand and turned to her daughter. He instantly missed her touch.

"Is she hungry?"

"No, just tired of being cooped up." Sidney lifted Lilly into her arms, so he could see the baby. "I'm afraid I have to go soon. I have a meeting with my insurance agent."

He swallowed a protest. "I wanted to help you through that."

"Well, you can help by getting better." Sidney met his gaze head-on. "You've been wonderful, Tanner. I want you to know how much I appreciate everything you've done for me."

That sounded suspiciously like a good-bye. He raised the head of his bed, so he could see her better. Her expression didn't reveal her thoughts. There was so much he wanted to say, but he didn't have the opportunity.

"Hey, look who's awake?" Colt entered the hospital room. "Glad to see you made it through, buddy."

"Yeah, me, too." Tanner watched with a flash of jealousy as Colt took Lilly from Sidney's arms and made funny faces at her.

"We'll check in on you later, okay?" Sidney moved away from his bed and grabbed her coat.

He didn't want them to go, but the pain in his side was growing worse by the minute. As Colt and Sidney left his room, he pressed the call button for the nurse.

And tried not to feel as if he'd just lost Sidney, forever.

* * *

"He looked so pale." Sidney had been taken aback by Tanner's wan appearance. The man who'd been so strong, so supportive through this nightmare, had taken a rough turn with this emergency surgery.

"He'll be fine, don't worry. He's too stubborn to stay down for long." Colt eyed her. "Are you sure you're up to meeting with the insurance adjuster today?"

"Yes, it needs to be done." Waiting for news of Tanner's condition had been agonizing, so she'd decided to take the same approach she had in law school. She'd made a list of everything she needed to accomplish. And the top priority was meeting with the insurance agent.

Followed by arranging new child care.

And then furnishing Lilly's room in her newly rented home.

Staying focused on the mundane didn't really help distract her from Tanner's injury and subsequent surgery. The thought of losing him forever had terrified her.

Even though, she knew full well she didn't have anything to offer him.

Sure, he was the kindest, most caring man she'd ever met. And his kisses made her feel alive for the first time since her divorce. But Tanner deserved a woman who wasn't approaching the ripe old age of thirty-seven. Her birthday wasn't until October, but still.

He deserved someone younger, someone who would give him the children he richly deserved.

The next twenty-four hours passed with agonizing slowness. The somewhat reassuring news she received was that Paul Kramer really did die of natural causes. Although she secretly thought the stress of Santiago's trial contributed to his heart attack.

But despite knowing Paul wasn't involved, she felt at odds. Colt was a nice guy, but he wasn't Tanner. This unhealthy yearning for Tanner had to stop. Sidney decided she'd go and see him in the morning one last time, then move on with her life.

Unfortunately, before she could ask Colt to take her to the hospital, she was called by yet another clerk, a woman named Fiona Kline, regarding a meeting request from defense counsel.

"I'll be there in thirty minutes." She disconnected from the phone. "Colt? I need to head to the courthouse."

"I thought we'd swing by the hospital first."

"I can't. The defense counsel wants to meet with me. Although if the news is what I think it is, we should be able to swing by afterward."

"Okay, that works." Colt waited as she packed Lilly's diaper bag, then bundled up the little girl.

She was early for the meeting, and wasn't surprised when Fiona mentioned Prosecutor Chance was present in the courtroom, as well.

Sidney pulled on her robe and entered

the courtroom. The two attorneys stood until she took her place behind the bench.

"I'd like this hearing to be on the record." Sidney gave the court reporter a nod. "Mr. Andrews? You requested this hearing."

"Yes, Your Honor." Quincy Andrews stood. He appeared far less arrogant than usual, his skin pale rather than his perpetual tan. "I had a long meeting with my client. Mr. Santiago is willing to change his plea to guilty in exchange for the prosecutor to take the death penalty off the table."

"Your Honor." Prosecutor Chance shot to his feet. "If anyone deserves the death penalty, it's Manual Santiago."

She glared at the prosecutor. "Mr. Chance, I'm in no mood for you to waste another moment of this court's time. You're being offered exactly what you wanted. A guilty plea."

"In addition," Andrews went on, "Mr. Santiago is willing to assist in giving law enforcement names of his criminal associates, including a private investigator who I used in the past for some legal work. I'm very upset to learn of this connection, Your Honor. And intend to sever ties with my client as soon as this is over."

Sidney didn't let on that she knew Wade Marcus was already in custody to testify against Santiago. She turned her attention back to the prosecutor. "Mr. Chance? Would you like to be heard?"

"I'll give Santiago life in prison without the possibility of parole," the prosecutor finally agreed. "But I want his full cooperation in bringing the rest of the cartel down."

"You'll have it," Andrews eagerly replied. "And we accept the deal."

"Good. Motion carried. This case has been dismissed. Fiona, remove all the calendar holds related to this matter, and release all potential jurors." She pounded her gavel and stood. "Thank you, gentlemen."

When she returned to her chambers, she found Colt on his phone. "Hold on, Tanner. Don't do anything foolish. We'll be there soon, okay?"

Alarm shot through her. "What's wrong?"

Colt shoved his phone in his pocket with a scowl. "Apparently he wants to leave the hospital against medical advice."

"Why on earth would he do that?" Sidney shrugged out of her robes and pulled on her coat. "I don't understand."

"I'm not sure, either, but I suspect it has something to do with you." Colt reached for Lilly's car seat.

"Me?" That hardly helped clear things up for her. It didn't make any sense. She quickly followed Colt through the courthouse, and out to his vehicle. Minutes later, they were on the road heading to the hospital.

When they arrived, Colt helped by carrying Lilly's car seat. She walked ahead, knowing the way to Tanner's room by heart.

It was a path she'd walked several times while waiting rather impatiently for news on his condition.

She knocked on his door, then eased it open. "Tanner? You decent?"

"Sidney?"

Pushing open the door, she was shocked to see him sitting on the edge of his bed, dressed in regular clothes. "What are you doing? You can't leave, you just had surgery!"

"I was coming to see you." Tanner sat with his hand pressed against his side. "I can't let you go."

"Let me go where?" She wondered if he was loopy from the pain meds. "Get back in your hospital gown, Tanner. You can't leave. I'm sure they want to keep you for a few days."

"Actually, the surgeon said he'd like to keep me for one more day, but the nurses tell me my vitals are good. So I'm not sure I need to stick around." Tanner's gaze searched hers. "I've been going nuts here by myself."

She glanced over her shoulder to see that Colt still had Lilly. He nodded at her, then stepped back into the hall and closed the door to give them privacy.

"I would have been here earlier, but I had to stop at the courthouse," she explained. "Santiago changed his plea to guilty, taking a sentence of life without parole and no death penalty. He's also willing to give names of his associates, which basically sealed the deal." She smiled widely. "The trial has been cancelled. It's over, Tanner."

"I'm thankful for that news," he said, his gaze never wavering from hers. "But I still wanted to see you. I grew worried, because yesterday you gave me the impression you were leaving forever."

Leaving him? Her heart squeezed in her chest. If she had her way, she'd never leave his side. But that couldn't be what he was talking about. "I'm not sure I understand what you mean. I live here in Cheyenne—where else would I go? I may not have a house of my own at the moment, but the rental you arranged is very nice."

"Not physically leaving town, but ending our relationship," he clarified. "I love you, Sidney." Tanner's blunt statement seemed to come out of left field. "I love Lilly, too, and I can't bear the thought of losing you. Not when the two of you make my life worth living."

It was the sweetest thing any man had ever said to her, and Sidney longed to throw herself into his arms.

But she didn't. "Tanner, I care about you, too. In fact, I've come to appreciate how God sent you to help protect me and Lilly. But as far as a relationship goes, I'm several years older than you, and well…" She gulped, then bravely continued. "I can't have children. It's a medical issue that can't be changed. And it's the main reason I became a foster parent, hoping and praying for a baby to adopt. God gave me Lilly, a blessing I'm very grateful for. But you deserve better, a younger woman, someone who will gladly give you a family of your own."

"There isn't anyone better than you, Sidney." He stood with a grimace, taking a step toward her. "I don't want another woman. And why on earth does age matter, anyway? So what if there are a few years between us? All that matters is that I love you." He reached out to take her hand.

She wanted to be strong, but her resistance crumbled at the sheer hope and longing in his eyes. "Tanner..." she sighed, not sure what to say.

"I understand you may not feel the same way about me." Tanner tugged her toward him. "I can appreciate that we've only known each other a few months. But I want to be a part of your life, Sidney. Yours and Lilly's. All I'm asking is that you give a relationship between us a try. Starting with letting me support you through the adoption process. I want to be with you in court at the end of the month."

The way he included her daughter brought the threat of tears. Then she remembered how awful she felt watching him being wheeled away. How terrified she'd been that he might not survive the emergency surgery.

How she'd prayed for God to watch over Tanner, and to heal his wound.

"I love you, Tanner. But it feels selfish. If I were a few years younger, maybe…" She didn't finish because Tanner pulled her into his arms.

"That's all I needed to hear." His voice was low and husky, and shivers of awareness went down her spine. "Love is all that matters, Sidney." He kissed her, and couldn't stop herself from gently wrapping her arms around his neck, and hugging him without hurting him.

His kiss represented everything she'd

dreamed of. Hope. Happiness. Love. Honor. Respect.

How could she let him go?

When she needed to breathe, she broke off from his kiss and gazed up at him. "Tanner, I agree that love is all that matters. But I also don't want you to regret the ability to have a family of your own. A few years from now, you might feel differently."

"You and Lilly are the family I want and need." He offered a crooked smile. "I already love Lilly like a daughter, and I think she likes me, too. I promise to be there for you both, whenever you need me. I know my job involves travel, but I'm going to make changes, the way Slade did, so that I don't have to be gone as much. And with my injury, I'll be sidelined for a while, anyway. Plus I have lots of vacation time."

"Tanner, I don't want you to change your career for me."

"I would change it for us, but that's

something we can figure out later. We were talking about family, about children. I'm sure there's another little boy out there who needs a home. Or another girl. Or one of each. It doesn't matter to me, as long as you're happy."

Three? He wanted three children? She could barely wrap her mind around it. Then he was kissing her again, making her realize the number was irrelevant.

Love really was all that mattered. And that's what she had right here with him.

A blessing she'd cherish for the rest of their lives.

EPILOGUE

Valentine's Day...

Tanner tugged at the tuxedo that was strangling him. "Why is Slade punishing us by making us wear these monkey suits, anyway?"

"Uh, because it's his wedding day?" Colt shook his head. "Stop complaining, I've noticed Sidney can't keep her eyes off you. You might want to invest in buying one, as it seems she likes the way you look in a tux."

Tanner grinned and stopped tugging at the collar. "She's beautiful, isn't she? I'm the one who can't stop looking at her."

"Okay, enough." Colt rolled his eyes.

"Between you and Slade I've had just about all the romance I can take."

Tanner clapped him on the back. "Your turn is coming."

Colt shook his head, all signs of mirth gone. "Not happening. Let's go join the reception."

They walked into the hall, and Tanner's gaze instantly found Sidney. She wore a stunning red dress that he personally thought may have overshadowed the bride. Robyn had been gorgeous, but Sidney stole his breath.

He crossed over and caught her hand in his. "May I have this dance?"

She blushed and nodded. "The wedding was wonderful, wasn't it?"

"Yeah." He knew Slade and Robyn had been through a lot, but today their love shone true. "Thanks for attending this shindig with me."

"Thanks for inviting me."

He pulled her closer and spun in a circle, making her laugh. Sidney's adoption of Lilly had been finalized and she had found a new nanny, Martha, who was currently watching Lilly. "Have you decided on a number yet?"

"Tanner." Sidney let out an exaggerated sigh. This was an ongoing discussion between them. "We can't discuss more children at this point in our relationship."

"That's what I thought you'd say." He abruptly stopped dancing, went down on one knee right there in the middle of Slade's reception and pulled out a ring. "Sidney, will you do me the honor of marrying me?"

Sidney's eyes widened in shock, but then her features filled with joy. All the other couples on the dance floor stopped to watch, including Slade and Robyn, and his boss, James Crane, and Lucille Lowry.

"I love you, and I love Lilly and I will love all the other children who need us. Please be my wife?"

"Yes, Tanner." She let out a laugh, her

cheeks turning pink at being the center of attention. "Yes, I'll marry you. Now stand up, this is Slade and Robyn's wedding day."

"We don't mind," Robyn assured her, smiling broadly. "In fact, welcome to the family, Sidney."

"I mind," Crane groused. "I'm losing good marshals faster than I can replace them."

"Not losing," Slade corrected. "Reassigning."

Ignoring them, Tanner rose and took the ring from the box, sliding it onto the fourth finger of Sidney's left hand. It was a little big, but not by much. He kissed her fingers, then drew her into his arms. "Thanks for making me the happiest man on the planet."

"Oh, Tanner." She reached up to kiss him. "I'm so glad God brought us together."

"Me, too." He smiled down at her. "Okay,

now that we are official engaged, have you decided on a number?"

She burst out laughing. "Obsessed with children, are you? Okay, here's my number." She went up on her tiptoes and whispered, "Five."

"Five?" His voice came out in a high embarrassing squeak. "Really?"

She laughed again. "No, silly, but you should have seen the look on your face. Priceless."

He was still grappling with the idea of five kids. "So then, how many?"

"How about we just take them one at a time?" She kissed him again. "And leave the number up to God."

"I can live with that." He spun her around again, his heart full of love and hope for their future.

And for the blessings God has bestowed upon them.

* * * * *

If you enjoyed this book, don't miss these other stories from Laura Scott:

Shielding His Christmas Witness
The Only Witness
Christmas Amnesia
Shattered Lullaby
Primary Suspect
Protecting His Secret Son
Soldier's Christmas Secrets
Guarded by the Soldier
Wyoming Mountain Escape
Hiding His Holiday Witness

Available now from
Love Inspired Suspense!
Find more great reads at
www.LoveInspired.com

Dear Reader,

I hope you enjoyed Tanner and Sidney's story in Rocky Mountain Standoff. Researching the US Marshals has been fun and I've really enjoyed creating these characters for my Justice Seekers series. I hope you've come to love them, too. Currently, I'm working on Colt's story. You didn't think I'd leave him out in the cold, did you? I hope you agree he deserves a happily-ever-after of his own.

I adore hearing from my readers! I can be reached through my website at www. laurascottbooks.com, through Facebook at https://www.facebook.com/LauraScott-Books and Twitter at https://twitter.com/ laurascottbooks. For up-to-date news on my new releases, consider signing up for my monthly newsletter. Not only do all subscribers get a free novella not available for purchase, but you'll hear as soon as the next Justice Seeker book is available for your reading pleasure.

Until next time,
Laura Scott